HER HEART'S TREASURE

Other books by Cathy McDavid:

His Desert Rose

HER HEART'S
TREASURE

•

Cathy McDavid

AVALON BOOKS
NEW YORK

PRINTED IN THE UNITED STATES OF AMERICA
ON ACID-FREE PAPER
BY HADDON CRAFTSMEN, BLOOMSBURG, PENNSYLVANIA

To my late grandfather, Edward Chapdelaine,
whose adventures as a young man in Arizona were,
in small part, my inspiration for this story.

And to my husband Kevin for planting the story-seed
when he took me to Bisbee and showed me an old
photograph of a mule being lowered into a mine shaft.

Prologue

October 16, 1906

There are those who say the Silver Angel Mine is nothing more than a legend; a story told by Indian elders around late night campfires. They say the Jesuit Priests chose the Mano del Diablo *Mountains to build their mission because of the lush valley and the river which runs through it, not because a vein of silver flowed deep within the cliffs that rise from the ground in the shape of a giant fist. They say, don't waste your life chasing impossible dreams. Go work for the Paradise Consolidated Copper Company. There, you can make money instead of throwing it away.*

There are also those who say the Jesuit Priests did more than bring the word of God to a primitive and uneducated people. They say the holy men claimed the precious ore and used it to build their mission, trading with the Indians for labor and materials. They say the

1

Silver Angel Mine is not legend, but fact, and I believe them. I need simply to hold the old ring in my hand to know the stories are true.

There is a treasure of untold value hidden in the Mano del Diablo *Mountains. The only question is: Where?*

Charles Oliver Bidwell

Chapter One

Paradise, Arizona
July, 1915

A shrill scream erupted from deep within the main shaft of number twenty-seven, ricocheted off the cold, damp walls, and speared Mercy Bidwell straight through the heart. Panic set her feet in motion, and she stumbled forward, arms flailing. The toe of her high-button boot caught on the rocky floor of the tunnel, and she pitched forward, nearly falling. From the shadowy recesses, slender, hook-like fingers gripped her by the elbow and firmly yanked her back.

"You'd best wait here, Miss," ordered a gruff voice. "Your uncle'll skin me alive if anything happens to you, and I've grown mighty fond of my skin over the years."

Mercy glanced at the small, wiry man detaining her. She recognized him as one of the miners and knew he meant her no harm.

"Let me go." She tugged in vain to separate herself from his surprisingly strong hold. "They're hurting him."

3

"They ain't hurtin' that miserable cuss." He spit off to the side, then wiped his mouth on the back of his shirt sleeve. "Scarin' the hair off his hide, maybe—but they ain't hurtin' him."

"How can you be sure?" Mercy didn't wish to appear rude by questioning the man, but she'd never heard an animal make such a blood-curdling noise except in the throes of death.

"Two Names is a tough ole goat. He'll come through just fine."

She frowned with anxiety. "Two Names? I thought he was called Samson."

The man gave a hearty chuckle. "We miners have a second name for that one."

"Oh? And what is it?"

His chuckle rapidly dissolved into a cough, followed by a throat-clearing. "Well, it ain't exactly fittin' for proper ladies to hear, if you catch my drift."

"I see."

Before Mercy could say more, another scream rose from the shaft, followed by a terrible clatter and a chorus of angry shouts. The commotion momentarily distracted her self-appointed guard and allowed her to escape. He may have been strong, but a bum right leg prevented him from giving much of a chase. Mercy made it all the way to the shaft opening before she was stopped again—this time by the mine superintendent himself, her uncle, Artemis.

Wheeling on her, he thundered, "What in tarnation are you doing here, girl? You know the rules. Only miners are allowed in the tunnels." He pointed back the way she'd come. "Now get out of here before I forget you're a grown woman and take you over my knee."

Mercy retreated a step, watching the proceedings with interest.

Several men were stationed around the opening of the mine shaft. A series of cables criss-crossed overhead, winding around pulleys suspended from the ceiling. The cables were joined to a large cylinder with handles on each side. Two men operated the cylinder. The others managed the cables, insuring they didn't become tangled or twisted.

Shouting orders to one another as they labored, they slowly and strenuously raised their live cargo from the lower level tunnels—the cargo Mercy's uncle had promised would be hers.

"I thought I told you to leave."

"I won't get in the way, Uncle." She simply *had* to be present when they pulled Samson from the mine shaft. "I promise I'll stay put and not utter a single sound." Moving to stand by an empty ore cart, she assumed a meek stance.

Artemis Bidwell rolled his eyes. "That'll be the day."

He had good reason to doubt his niece. Mercy didn't know the meaning of the word "meek." Her father, Charles Oliver Bidwell, had thought of her as his precocious, darling daughter. The teachers at Boston Academy for Young Women, where she'd been nearly expelled on numerous occasions, were less kind in their observations. Frequent notations of willful and insolent behavior, along with stern recommendations on how to improve, had regularly appeared in Mercy's academic records. The few young men who'd been brave or curious enough to come courting quickly shied away, her independent nature evidently not to their liking.

Sensing her uncle on the brink of acquiescing, Mercy batted her lashes and employed her most beguiling wiles. "Please, Uncle Artemis."

He gave in, as she hoped he would.

"You move one inch from that spot," he said, wagging a finger at her, "and the deal's off. You hear me?"

"Yes, I hear you."

"I have half a mind to send that mule right back where he came from. No *if*'s, *and*'s, or *but*'s about it." Uncle Artemis turned his back on her to watch over the men. "I don't know how I let you talk me into this. That beast is stone blind and crippled to boot—no good to anyone."

Except me, thought Mercy, relief washing over her. "You have my word. I won't move."

And she didn't. For almost one whole minute.

Another scream, this one closer and louder, exploded from the mouth of the shaft. More shouting, machinery grinding, and the wild thrashing of hooves against rock created a ruckus that filled the dank, ill-lit cavern to bursting. Without thinking, Mercy abandoned her post and stormed past her uncle, between the men, and right to the edge of shaft. There, she came to a sudden and dizzying stop, her heart trapped in her throat.

She'd never been this close to the shafts before. The huge opening loomed in front of her, pitch black and seemingly bottomless. A blast of cold, stale air struck her in the face. Disorientated, she closed her eyes and teetered slightly.

"Get back from there before you break your neck!" roared a male voice.

An arm reached out and locked around Mercy's waist. In the next instant, she was hauled off her feet and deposited a good ways back from the shaft opening. The arm didn't immediately release her, but instead held her firmly against a towering, solidly built frame.

For the first time in her twenty-two-and-one-half years, Mercy found herself wrapped in a man's embrace. Even in her muddled state of mind, she realized it was not an entirely unpleasant experience.

"Are you all right?" Dark eyes bored straight into hers.

"Yes, I think so."

Her knees felt ridiculously weak. If she didn't know better, she'd swear she was suffering heart palpitations—but that couldn't be. Mercy didn't swoon over men, even if they were young, strong, and exceedingly handsome. With his black, curly hair, impressive height, and chiseled features, Edward Cartier distinguished himself among the men of the Paradise Consolidated Copper Company—and not solely for his looks.

She knew his name. Few people in Paradise weren't acquainted with the Quebec farmer turned mining foreman, by reputation if nothing else. From what Mercy had gathered in the four months since she'd arrived in the remote desert mining community, Edward Cartier had earned himself a sizeable, and somewhat colorful, reputation.

"You'd best be careful, *Mademoiselle* Bidwell. The mines are no place for a woman to be rushing around . . . how do you say? Willy-nilly?"

She liked his accent. The way he softened consonants and lengthened vowels was pleasing to the ears. "I . . . I . . . didn't think. Thank you for rescuing me."

The noise, the men, the mule, everything around them faded into the background as their eyes met again and held. Something in his gaze intensified. Mercy responded with a quickening in her middle. Her hands found the front of his worn, blue chambray shirt and lightly rested there. The material, washed many times over to a velvety softness, tickled her fingertips.

"*Mon pleasure.*"

Mercy didn't speak French, but she guessed at the meaning of his words and the quickening in her middle increased, spreading outward so that her entire body hummed.

Uncle Artemis came at them, breaking the spell. "Mercy," he barked. "What in the name of God's green earth do you think you're doing?" He pulled at his thinning hair as if to rip it from his scalp, then came to an abrupt halt. His gaze fixed on Edward's arm and its location about Mercy's waist.

His tone took on an unmistakable steely quality. "I appreciate you rescuing my niece, Cartier, but I suggest you unhand her before I get the wrong impression."

Edward complied so quickly that Mercy stumbled backwards. With a small gasp, she fell neatly into her uncle's arms.

The clattering of hooves echoed through the tunnels, as did the screaming, which Mercy now recognized as the frightened bray of her soon-to-be charge.

"Begging your pardon, Mr. Bidwell," said one of the men operating the cylinder. The cables strung across the shaft opening shook violently. "This mule will be going to meet his maker right quick if we don't get him topside."

"And he'll take all of us with him," said his partner. Sweat coated his neck and stained his shirt.

Uncle Artemis whirled about and made a lifting motion with his hands. "Well? What are you waiting for? Bring the rascal up."

"One . . . two . . . three . . . heave."

Edward led the count and by doing so, kept Mercy's attention fixed on him. Her peculiar heart palpations continued, which she assured herself had not a single thing whatsoever to do with the broad shoulders stretching the material of Edward's shirt tight across his back.

Only when her uncle spoke did she tear her gaze away.

"Here he comes, boys. Watch it. He'd just as soon strike you as look at you."

A pair of long, brown ears appeared first. Next came two wild eyes, then a set of flaring nostrils. This time when Samson brayed, Mercy covered her own ears. He must have sensed the approach of solid ground because his front legs beat like twin pistons, seeking purchase.

When she saw the harness used to secure Samson for his ascent, Mercy was consumed with pity. She almost wished she hadn't insisted her uncle give her the mule and instead let him die in the lower level tunnels, as was his fate until she'd intervened. No one, not even an old and crippled animal, should be subjected to such torture.

"Mort, get under him," shouted Edward, reaching for the straps binding Samson's chest, "and help me pull."

"Have you lost your mind?" Mort shouted back. "The son of a buck will kill me."

Edward ignored the man's objections and placed himself in the direct path of Samson's slashing hooves. "Thomas, you and Guillermo get behind him and push when I give the signal."

Guillermo crossed himself and mouthed a silent prayer before getting in position. Thomas merely shrugged.

"Ready . . . set . . . now!"

Samson, for once, cooperated with his emancipators. The moment his front feet touched solid ground, he scrambled forward, almost trampling Edward in the process. Mercy's hands flew to her mouth. Uncle Artemis shoved Mort aside and grabbed the side of Samson's halter, jerking hard.

"Be careful." She rushed ahead, then stopped, knowing that this time her uncle wouldn't tolerate her interference. She made the right decision.

"Stay back, girl. I mean it."

With one last effort on the part of both men and mule, Samson clambered topside and righted himself. Head high, ears alert, he looked about with milky blue eyes. What he saw was anybody's guess. Years in the black tunnels had long ago robbed him of his sight.

When it appeared he wasn't going to bolt, the men stood back and gave him room, Uncle Artemis maintaining his hold on the halter. Samson shook himself from head to tail. The harness rattled and, without the tension of the lines to keep it in place, slid sideways. Then, as if this were nothing more than an ordinary day, he lowered his head to the ground and sniffed, shooting small clouds of dirt into the air.

"Well, fancy that." Uncle Artemis chuckled. "The rascal's already making himself at home."

Guillermo wiped his brow with a red handkerchief he'd pulled from the back pocket of his pants. "It is much easier lowering the *mulas* into the tunnels than bringing them up, no?"

Edward clapped the Mexican on the back. "*Oui, mon ami.* Much easier."

Mercy couldn't stand the waiting another moment. "Can I take him outside now?"

She walked slowly toward Samson, as much to keep from spooking him as to marvel at her acquisition. To everyone else, he was an old mule, past his prime and slated for the glue factory. To Mercy, he represented the second step in the realization of a dream. The first step had been finding her late father's journal tucked away in his belongings.

It had required all her powers of persuasion to convince her Uncle to give her the mule, and Mercy felt more than a little guilty at having lied to him. Well, not *lied* exactly— *exaggerated* was a better description. She did hate seeing poor, helpless animals suffer. She did want to treat Samson's afflictions and make a pet out of him. However, she also had another use in mind for him. One that involved hauling a wagon full of prospecting equipment to the nearby *Mano del Diablo* Mountains.

"I'd better take him, just in case," Uncle Artemis said, hooking a lead rope to Samson's halter. "Mort, give me a hand removing the harness."

Ready, willing and able to help—now that the potential for danger had passed—Mort jumped right in. "Be careful, Mr. Bidwell. They don't call him Two Names for nothing."

While the men saw to the harness removal, Mercy introduced herself to Samson. In anticipation, she'd brought a withered apple with her. She took it from her skirt pocket and held it to the mule's nose. His head snapped back, then inched forward cautiously. Apparently satisfied the apple presented no threat, he opened his mouth and took a bite. Before he'd even finished with what he had, he nosed Mercy's hand in search of more.

She gladly gave it to him. "Not so fast," she crooned and patted the side of his neck. "There's more where that came from."

"Spoiling him already?" Edward materialized at her side.

Mercy smiled. It was easier to relax around him with a mule and four other men providing a buffer. "I think a decade of service in the mines has earned him a little spoiling."

"Your uncle must care for you very much."

"Yes, he does." Her curiosity piqued, she peered at him from the corner of her eye. "But what makes you say that?"

"Because the mules only go down into the tunnels. They never come up."

What Edward said was true, and Mercy felt a renewed sense of guilt at having manipulated her uncle. "I am very grateful to him."

"All finished?" Uncle Artemis passed the last piece of harness to Mort, who carried it to a storage room off the main shaft opening.

Impulsively, Mercy threw herself at her uncle and kissed his cheek soundly.

"Whoa! What's that for?"

"Thank you. For everything. I'm sorry to be such a nuisance."

He smiled down at her fondly. "Sometimes, you remind me so much of your father."

She kissed his cheek again, tenderly this time. "I'll take that as a compliment."

He grumbled and swiped his hands together as if he couldn't be bothered with such silly sentimentality.

Mercy knew better.

"What say we get this rascal out of here." Uncle Artemis checked his pocketwatch. "It's already past one o'clock. These men need to get back to work and I have some requisitions on my desk to approve."

Behind them, a cage rattled to the top of the shaft and came to a stop.

The door opened and a man's head popped out. "Has Mr. Bidwell left yet?"

"I'm here."

"Mr. Bidwell," the man said when he caught sight of Uncle Artemis. "We need you on level one. A wall in that new tunnel we're digging has caved in."

"Anyone hurt?"

"No, but there's a lot of damage to the structure."

Uncle Artemis looked around. His eyes fell on Edward. "Take this mule for my niece, and don't let her get hurt. Do you understand?"

Edward nodded. "I will see to it."

Uncle Artemis hurried off, leaving Mercy and the mule in Edward's care. She didn't exactly like the arrangement, but then again, she wasn't in a position to argue.

"Shall we go?" she asked.

"After you."

Samson lumbered stiffly alongside Edward. Mercy winced. She'd known the mule was crippled, but she didn't realize how badly. Her first task after settling him into his new home, a small stock pen behind the mining offices where she worked as secretary for her uncle, would be to find the cause of his lameness and treat it.

She and Edward didn't talk much. Quite frankly, she was at a loss for what to say to him. Casual remarks such as, *is it true you were once a member of the Riverside Gang*, or, *Mort Carmichael told Sara Jane Ketchem you left Quebec because of a woman*, made for poor conversation. Mercy didn't put much stock in the rumors circulating about Edward Cartier and figured two-thirds of them, if not more, were pure fabrication. But which third wasn't?

As they neared the main opening, early afternoon sunlight spilled in, illuminating the tunnel. Samson suddenly balked. Facing the opening, he brayed loudly.

"What is it?" Mercy placed her hand on the mule's neck in an effort to calm him.

"The outside," Edward said. "He hasn't seen it in over ten years."

"I thought he was blind."

"Yes, but maybe not totally blind. Who knows for sure? His other senses tell him what his eyes cannot." Edward jerked on the lead rope. "Come along, *homme vieil.*"

Samson refused to budge. He brayed again, pawing the ground impatiently. Edward jerked harder.

"Come along, I say. There is nothing out there that will hurt you." Edward and Samson engaged in a tug-of-war battle. Samson won.

"I see now how he acquired his other name." Mercy couldn't help grinning. She didn't know which of them was more stubborn.

"I have a few names for him myself."

"Here. Let me try."

"You?"

"Yes, me."

Edward shot her an incredulous look. "You think you can get this mule to follow you?"

"I can't do any worse than you." She raised her chin.

"Be my guest." Mouth twitching, he handed her the lead rope, stood back and crossed his arms over his chest.

Mercy stroked Samson's velvety nose. Then, holding onto the halter, she stood on tiptoes and whispered in his ear. He lowered his head and shook it. When he raised it back up, she again whispered in his ear.

The mule took a tentative step forward. Then another.

Mercy smiled smugly and set off, leading the mule out of the tunnel and into the sunlight.

Edward caught up and matched her stride. "Well done. What did you say to him?"

"Nothing much. I told him I had more apples waiting for him at the stock pen and that I would take good care of him."

"And he understood?"

"Apparently." Mercy kept a straight face. Inside, she was laughing.

"I do not believe you," Edward scoffed, but his eyes twinkled with amusement. "It was a trick."

"I'll never tell." It *was* a trick, one her father had taught her as a little girl when her pony refused to cross a creek. He'd explained how blowing in an animal's ear would distract or annoy them enough to take a step, and one step was usually enough.

Another few minutes of silence passed, more comfortable than the first. It took a good fifteen minutes to walk the dirt road leading from the mines to the company buildings at the bottom of the hill. On a summer day like today, with the temperature reaching a hundred and twelve, Mercy would soon be bathed in perspiration. Workers passed them on the road coming and going. Some were on foot, others were on horseback or in wagons. One of the company's shiny black Model T Ford automobiles passed them, carrying a crew of engineers.

"What will you do with him?" Edward asked. He'd been quietly contemplating the panoramic view of the valley below. Samson walked between them, his hooves kicking up dust and sending small stones skipping in every direction.

"He's just a pet." Mercy stammered only once while answering. Because lying didn't come easy for her, she'd practiced her responses in order to sound natural. She had no intention of telling anyone her true plans for the mule. Not yet, anyway. Her late father's obsessive search for the Silver Angel Mine had made him the laughing stock of Paradise. She didn't wish for a similar fate.

"Why not a dog? A dog is less trouble than a mule."

"I have a soft spot for sick and injured animals."

His dark eyes smouldered as they stared into hers. "Yes, I believe you do."

Mercy tripped and momentarily lost her balance. No man had ever looked at her with such intensity before. To say the least, it was disquieting.

Edward continued walking. He either didn't notice her distress or he blamed the heat. "With a small amount of training, the mule can still earn his keep. He may be blind, but there is no reason he cannot pull a wagon or buggy once his leg is healed."

Her stomach dropped a foot. Edward's comment hit too close to home for comfort. And if he'd figured her out that easily, so might her uncle, who would surely put a stop to her plans.

"Why would I ever need him to pull a wagon?" she trilled in a high voice.

He gave her a curious stare. "Perhaps you have a secret purpose."

Drat! He was onto her. She tried putting him off by playing along. "So what if I do? Haven't you ever had a secret purpose, Sir?"

"Yes. I have one now, in fact." His tone hinted at a double meaning. "One that is very near and dear to me."

Mercy gulped. This was not going at all the way she'd intended. She'd best put a stop to it before he got the wrong impression of her.

"I'm afraid I can't be any part of whatever it is you're plotting, Mr. Cartier."

One corner of his mouth quirked up in a disarming smile. "I do not remember saying you were."

"Then you . . . it wasn't . . ." To Mercy's horror, her cheeks flamed and, as she often did when flustered, she lost her temper. "You deliberately let me think your secret purpose included me."

"I did no such thing. You assumed."

Mercy started to reply, but Edward cut her off. Not with any remark, but rather with the deliberate step he took toward her. She would have retreated if her shoes had not become mysteriously rooted to the ground.

"I am not unhappy you assumed my secret purpose involves you," he said in a low voice that reminded Mercy of the soft breeze which blows right before a rainfall. "The idea has merit. Great merit."

Chapter Two

I met an old Pima Indian and his granddaughter today. After introductions were made, I asked them to join my campfire. The young woman spoke English quite well and acted as translator for her grandfather. She told me she was taking him to stay with relatives on the reservation near Phoenix. On impulse, I showed them the ring, indicating the angel engraving on top. The old man looked as if he'd seen a ghost, and his granddaughter cowered in fear.

The old man asked me where I got the ring. I told him a rancher just north of here sold it to me and insisted it once belonged to a Jesuit Priest from the mission. The old man waved a shaky finger at the ring and started rambling. He called the ring Angel de Plata, *which is Spanish for "Silver Angel." Before I could ask how a Pima Indian knew a Spanish word, he said his grandfather's grandfather had been one of the*

17

Indians to help the holy men build the mission and mine the silver. This ancestor had also been among the party of warriors who rose up and killed the holy men after years of abuse and mistreatment. I asked the old man if he knew where the Silver Angel Mine was, and he just stared at the night sky.

Then the oddest thing happened. The young woman's eyes glassed over, and she became quite still. In a peculiar voice, not of this world, she said, "There is a bad spirit which resides in the Angel de Plata. *Do not go in. If you do, you will never come out alive."*

Suddenly, an icy chill crept over me and when I looked down, my arms were completely covered in goose bumps.

Charles Oliver Bidwell

Mercy squeezed Samson's lead rope, trying her best to concentrate. What little she'd eaten for supper churned uncomfortably in her stomach, and a persistent restlessness nagged at her as if a small insect crawled up her leg.

Curse Edward Cartier. This was all his fault.

Every time she thought of him, she bit her bottom lip to stop from screaming in frustration. She was mad. Hopping mad. Not at him, but at herself and her foolish schoolgirl reaction to his flirting. She hadn't been able to get him out of her mind all afternoon, and that wasn't like her. True, Mercy had little experience with the opposite sex, but neither did she lack confidence when socializing with them—until Edward.

No! She must stop thinking of him.

Forcing her gaze downward, she watched Frosty run his gnarled hand along Samson's front legs. If the mule's lameness proved beyond treatment, her plans to take up where her father left off would be delayed until she acquired another animal capable of pulling a wagon. It would be a nearly impossible task. Uncle Artemis would hardly believe she wanted two mules as pets. She'd have no choice but to purchase one, and the trip from Boston to Paradise four months earlier had depleted her entire savings.

Frosty stood, stroking his full white beard. That, along with a matching head of thick white hair, had given him his nickname. Mercy never asked her late father's prospecting partner about his real name. She couldn't imagine calling him anything except the nickname.

She interrupted his reverie, unable to wait another moment. "What's wrong with him?"

"I'm no expert, mind you, but it appears to me he has a stone bruise on the underside of that right hind hoof."

"A stone bruise? Are you sure?" She phrased her question politely, not wishing to insult Frosty. "His limp is rather severe."

"It's likely abscessed, what with the hoof being so hot and all." Samson nosed Frosty's battered felt hat, knocking it sideways. The wizened old-timer ignored him. "I reckon, because of him being past his prime and blind, no one bothered to treat it."

"Can he be cured?" Mercy held her breath.

So much depended on Frosty's answer. If all went as planned, she would find the Silver Angel Mine, thus proving to the skeptics that her dear father hadn't been crazy. Then she'd utilize her newfound wealth to leave Paradise and her dreary, miserable life behind forever.

Mercy hadn't always been unhappy. Until her twelfth year, she'd enjoyed an idyllic childhood. Then her mother unexpectedly died of a fever and her grief-stricken father, unable to cope with the loss, enrolled Mercy in boarding school. Soon after, he embarked on a string of adventures, which ended—or began, depending on how one looked at it—in Paradise with the search for the Silver Angel Mine.

"Cured?" Frosty straightened his crooked hat, then patted Samson. The two had become fast friends. "I don't rightly know, but we can sure enough try."

"Oh." Disappointment washed over Mercy.

"Now don't go getting all sad-faced on me. We ain't beat yet." He lifted Mercy's chin with his finger. "Your pa, he didn't give up none too easily. I ain't never seen a more persistent man."

At the reference to her father, Mercy squared her shoulders. "Tell me what to do."

"Know how to make a poultice?"

She nodded.

"Good. Twice a day, soak his hoof in a bucket of hot water." Frosty walked around to the mule's hind end and Mercy followed, still holding the lead rope. "Pack the inside hoof with the poultice, then wrap it with a cloth and tie it in place. Burlap works well if you have any."

"There's some in the warehouse."

"Watch he don't kick you." Frosty ran a hand down Samson's back leg and picked up the afflicted hoof. "He's acting well enough, but you can't be too careful.

"I'll watch him," Mercy said with more assurance than she felt. Already she was searching her mind for someone she could recruit to assist her.

"Once the abscess drains, you'll need to get him properly shoed or all your hard work'll be for nothing."

Mercy wondered dismally what the farrier charged for his services, and where else she could cut corners. "When are you leaving?"

"Morning, at the crack of dawn." He gave her a smile that managed to be encouraging, despite a number of missing teeth. Frosty's visits to town lasted no longer than a day or two. After a quick swapping of gold ore for necessities, he'd head out again. "But I'll be back in a week or two. It'll take that long for this fellow to heal, and for you to round up the rest of the supplies we need."

That long, or possibly longer. The quest for riches, Mercy was fast learning, required riches to begin with. There was so much to buy before beginning her search for the mine. In addition to a dependable animal to pull a wagon, she needed a wagon for him to pull—not to mention tools, rope, canteens, canvas tarpaulins, lanterns. The list was endless.

"Are you sure you want to go through with this?" Frosty asked, not unkindly. "Late summer ain't the best season for prospecting, on account of it's hot as blue blazes. Then there's the rain to think about. Now me, I'm used to it—but a city girl like you ain't."

Mercy mustered her resolve. "I'll manage."

"Manage what exactly, may I ask?"

They turned simultaneously. At the sight of the interloper, Mercy's churning stomach twisted into a knot. "Uncle Artemis!" How long had he been standing there, and how much had he heard? Evidently, enough.

"What's going on here?"

He approached, and Mercy retreated a step, bumping into Samson's side. She'd forgotten how imposing her uncle could be, much like her father. Height had less to do with it than presence. Artemis Bidwell wielded a tremendous amount of responsibility and wore it well. All the men, from the lowliest laborer to the most senior foreman, respected him.

"Frosty was looking at Samson for me. He thinks there's a stone bruise on his hoof and that's why he's limping." It wasn't a lie, Mercy told herself, crossing two fingers and hiding them behind her back.

Uncle Artemis gave her the look that reduced many a stalwart miner to a babbling idiot. It had the same effect on her.

"We were talking . . . uh . . . about Frosty's next trip into the . . . uh . . . mountains."

Uncle Artemis advanced another step. Mercy gulped, but stood her ground. Frosty, on the other hand, tried to slip discretely away.

"Hold it right there, Frosty."

Frosty came to an abrupt halt and had the good sense to remove his hat. "Of course, Mr. Bidwell."

Uncle Artemis's eyes went from one to the other. He folded his arms across his barrel chest and said, "It's clear you two are in the middle of devising some plan. Care to enlighten me?"

Money had just become the least of Mercy's worries. "Not really."

"That wasn't a request."

She mentally debated her options, then chose to come clean. Sooner or later she'd have to tell her uncle, so she might as well get it over with while reinforcements were at hand.

After several false starts, she blurted, "Frosty's agreed to help me continue Father's search for the Silver Angel Mine."

Uncle Artemis stared at her, dumbstruck. His expression, however, spoke volumes, changing from shock, to disbelief, to anger.

"I forbid it," he said at last.

She fiddled nervously with the lead rope. Samson appeared to have dozed off, and Frosty picked at a piece of lint on his shirt. So much for reinforcements.

"I wish you wouldn't do that," Mercy said carefully.

"You *wish* I wouldn't do that?"

"Yes, sir." She breathed deeply, drawing on the same courage which had served her in the recent past when, scared and on her own for the first time, she'd climbed aboard a train headed for Arizona. "Because I'm going whether you approve or not. I love you and Aunt Connie," she hurried on when he started to comment, "and I appreciate all you've done for me, taking me in, giving me a home and a job. But finding the Silver Angel Mine is important to me—the most important thing in my life."

"You have no experience," he said sharply. "No equipment, no supplies, no business whatsoever going off into the mountains. Look what happened to your father."

"Frosty will help me, and I have Samson."

Uncle Artemis clutched the sides of his head as if in terrible pain. "An old man and a blind, crippled mule. Good Lord, Mercy, you can't be serious."

She bristled at his criticism. "I'm very serious."

"You don't even know where to start looking."

"But I do! I have Father's journal. It was with his things, if you remember. He specifically mentions the location of the mine; the east rim of the *Mano del Diablo* Mountains, at the base of the third finger."

"The mine is a myth." Uncle Artemis sighed tiredly. "It never existed."

"It does." Mercy's right hand went automatically to the heavy silver ring she always wore on a chain around her neck. The cool metal burned her palm. "I have proof."

"That ring could have been made anywhere."

"But it wasn't. It was made here, by Indians who mined the silver for the priests." How could she defend something based entirely on faith and faith alone?

"Your father had that same conviction." Uncle Artemis's shoulders sagged. He closed his eyes and rubbed his forehead. When he next spoke, it was with tenderness rather than fury. "I miss him. You being here is almost like having him with us again." He took hold of Mercy's upper arms and gazed at her with affection. "I don't want to lose you, too."

Frosty took that moment to excuse himself. "If you don't mind, I'll just mosey along and give you two some privacy."

"Wait for me by the gate," she told him without looking away from her uncle. "I need you to show me how to soak Samson's foot."

"Mercy," her uncle warned.

She shrugged out of his hold. "Whatever the outcome of our argument, the mule's injury needs tending."

"We're not arguing, we're discussing," he said to her back.

Mercy grew quiet at the sight of Frosty untying Buttercup from the post where he'd left her. Every time she saw the sad-eyed little burro, her heart constricted. As the story went, Buttercup had carried her dead father's body down from the *Mano del Diablo* Mountains and through the desert to Paradise, where he'd received a proper funeral and burial. On that same day, twenty-seven hundred miles away, Mercy had been buying her train ticket, oblivious to what awaited her on the other end of her journey.

Frosty hadn't told her the story and neither had her uncle or his family. Mercy heard the gruesome details of her father's death from the town gossips who, it seemed, took perverse pleasure in seeing her react.

Facing her uncle, she made a last effort to reason with him. "I don't expect you to understand. I hardly understand this compulsion myself."

"Then, for pity's sake, drop it."

"I can't."

"You mean you refuse."

"It'll be night soon." Mercy gazed at the setting sun, a huge ball of fire just beginning to dip below the horizon. "And Frosty's waiting for me."

"Nice try, young lady, but changing the subject will only delay the inevitable." Uncle Artemis lowered his head until their noses were mere inches apart. "We're not done with this. Not by a long shot."

Edward made a conscious effort not to rush. Meetings with the mine superintendent weren't unusual, however private meetings with the mine superintendent in his office were. He told himself the summons didn't necessarily indicate a problem, but his gut disagreed.

In the nearly eleven months he'd been working for the Paradise Consolidated Copper Company, he'd been an exemplary employee, steadily advancing within the ranks as positions became available. He'd done it despite outlandish rumors regarding his personal life—or, perhaps, because of them.

Either way, he made the best of circumstances and used the awe his coworkers held him in to his advantage. He liked his job. More than that, he needed it. There were too many loved ones back home depending on him. Of all the places he'd worked since coming to America, none had offered the same stability or earning potential as Paradise. The war in Europe, for all its terrible aspects, had created a boon in the copper industry and provided hundreds of men with gainful employment.

He bounded up the steps to the front door of the mining office, his boots heavy on the wooden porch. He hesitated with his hand on the knob. It occurred to him, not for the first time since receiving the summons, that he might encounter another Bidwell. Perhaps one with honey-brown hair stacked in a loose bun on her head, green eyes vivid as desert fauna in spring, and a well-proportioned figure her rigid style of dress failed to conceal. Mercy Bidwell.

He'd recalled his encounter with the mine superintendent's lovely niece frequently over the past two days, and always with a smile. Edward liked women. It was one of the few rumors circulating about him that was based on fact. But he hadn't met a woman he liked as much as Mercy Bidwell in a very long time.

Not since Anne-Marie.

He still missed his late wife and thought of her often. After all, she'd given him a child—the greatest gift a woman could give a man. But deep down, Edward was a pragmatist. Life went on. He had a job to do and a family to feed. And while he'd always cherish his memories of Anne-Marie, he wouldn't live in the past. She wouldn't have wanted him to, either.

The door to the mining office creaked softly as he opened it, and Edward let himself in. Thick curtains covered the two small windows on either side of the room, in an effort to keep the sweltering heat at bay. Electric wall lamps took the place of sunlight, giving the room a strange, unnatural appearance. The effect was further enhanced by an odd, rhythmic, clacking sound.

It appeared to come from Mercy, who sat hunched over a roll-top desk. The desk itself was situated behind a long counter that ran the length of the office. A small gate at the end had been left open. To her right was a telephone switch-board, the wires crossing each other in a complex pattern which defied understanding.

Edward strode forward and was rewarded when she looked up, her expression slightly startled. She watched him cross the room, and he liked the interest—albeit wary interest—he saw reflected in her eyes. Reaching the counter, he casually rested his forearms on it. The source of the strange clacking sound became quickly apparent.

"*Bonjour, Mademoiselle* Bidwell." He tugged on the corner of his hat. "How are you this hot day?"

"Mister Cartier." She removed her hands from the type-writing machine and set them primly in her lap. "My uncle is expecting you, but he's currently on the telephone." She glanced at the switchboard, then back at Edward. "He won't be long, if you'd care to wait."

"I would be delighted to wait." He peered over the counter at the typewriting machine. "Interesting. I have never seen one of these up close. Tell me, where does one learn to operate such a complicated piece of machinery?"

"I attended school." Without looking at him, she began leafing through a stack of papers. "In Boston."

"Ah, of course." Edward grinned, undaunted by her prim and proper attitude. She may not realize that, as the mine superintendent's niece, she was safe from his advances—but that didn't stop him from engaging her in conversation. He enjoyed the high color in her cheeks too much to leave her alone.

"You can have a seat over there while you wait." She nodded at two straight-back chairs in the corner. "I'm sure my uncle will be finished shortly. I'll call you the second he's available."

Edward cranked the upper half of his body around, noted the distance between the chairs and his current place at the counter, then shook his head. "Thank you, but I prefer to wait here." He grinned again. "The smell of your cologne will not reach me over there. Lilac, is it not?"

"Oh!"

Her profuse blush captivated Edward completely and, for once, he found himself tongue-tied.

They were both spared when a side door flew open and Artemis Bidwell emerged, visibly stressed. "There you are, Cartier. Come in." He moved aside to let Edward pass. "Mercy, while I'm meeting with Mr. Cartier, I need you to telephone the governor's office. Let me know the moment you get through."

"Yes, sir." She lifted the telephone earpiece, placed it over her head and swivelled her chair around to face the switchboard, plugging and unplugging wires.

Artemis Bidwell closed his office door after Edward. "Have a seat," he said, motioning with an outstretched hand as he rounded a large oak desk in the middle of the room.

Edward complied and waited for his boss to come to the point of their meeting. He didn't have to wait long.

Once situated in his chair, Artemis Bidwell steepled his fingers and studied Edward. "I've been observing you closely since you started working for us, Cartier. You're a hard-working, ambitious man."

"That I am, Mr. Bidwell." Ambition meant advancement. Advancement meant increased wages and less family members going hungry.

"You're also trustworthy. That's a quality I admire. It's one that gets you ahead in this business." Artemis Bidwell reclined in his chair, his hands gripping the arm rests. "I have a proposition for you, one that promises to be lucrative if the outcome proceeds as I'd like it to. Are you interested?"

Edward leaned forward. "I am always interested in lucrative propositions."

"Good." The mine superintendent smiled with satisfaction. "This one involves my niece, Mercy, and the Silver Angel Mine."

Chapter Three

I discovered a drawing today, carved in the face of a rock halfway up the east rim of the third finger. The rock was almost entirely covered by shrub. Had I not decided to stop and rest in the exact spot I did, I would have walked right past it.

At first glance, the design made no sense, with its crooked lines and strange geometrical shapes. Yet, I sensed something familiar about it, something I couldn't quite put my finger on.

Frosty says the carving was done centuries ago by Indians, and has nothing whatsoever to do with the mine. There are ruins in the area; crumbling walls of stone pueblos once occupied by the Ancient Ones. They were known to make records of successful hunts or maps to hidden food stores. Still, I'm going to return tomorrow and study the carving further. There may be something I've missed.

*In the meantime, Frosty has a pot of coffee brewing.
There's a chill in the air. I can feel it clear to my bones.
A cup of hot coffee should chase it away—that, and
some good conversation. Besides being a better cook
than most women, Frosty is an excellent storyteller.*

*The last few years have been lonely. I didn't realize
how lonely until I took Frosty on as a partner. I'm glad
he's here with me. For some reason, I don't feel like
being by myself tonight.*

Charles Oliver Bidwell

Mercy stared at the array of equipment and supplies
stacked against the stable wall. Her uncle's generosity had
been limitless. He'd assembled everything she and Frosty
needed for their prospecting expeditions, right down to a
rickety farm wagon and worn leather harness. But there was
a string attached, one Mercy had yet to decide if she'd
accept or decline.

At the sound of footsteps behind her, she turned her head.
Her uncle was approaching and bringing the string with him.
Edward Cartier smiled and tipped his hat. Without warning,
Mercy's heart began to hammer, and she pinched herself on
the wrist to counteract the effects of his dangerous good
looks. She would not, under any circumstances, allow him to
get to her.

"They're here," she said in a low voice, so as not to be
heard by anyone except Frosty.

The old prospector crouched in front of a long wooden crate
containing a pickaxe, shovel, and various other tools. "You
don't say." He stood, bracing a hand on his bent knee. "I've
heard tell of this here Cartier. Some of it good, some of it bad."

"It's the bad part that has me worried," Mercy muttered,
then smiled sweetly at her uncle. "Good morning, sir."
Keeping her voice formal, she added, "Mr. Cartier."

"Ah, Mercy." Uncle Artemis opened his arms wide, and she went into them. He patted her as though she were a small child. "That's a good girl. Right on time."

She gritted her teeth. This act of his was for Edward's benefit as well as hers. Her uncle wanted her to appear helpless and in need of able-bodied assistance. He probably thought it would make her more willing to accept the condition he had placed on the loan of equipment and supplies; Edward's participation in her search for the mine.

"You know me. Always punctual."

"An admirable quality. Don't ever be ashamed of it."

Mercy eased away from her uncle. Part of her understood that he loved her and wanted to protect her. Part of her was angry at his efforts to control her. Did he not remember she'd traveled alone across the country, all the way from Boston to Paradise? She sighed inwardly. No matter the passing years, he still saw her as the little girl she'd once been, not the grown-up woman she'd become. Still, with both her parents gone, it was nice to have a family who cared. She'd missed that during her years at boarding school. Would it really be so terrible having Edward along? Especially if it made her uncle happy. He'd been so good to her.

She caught Edward staring at her, his dark eyes shining with the same intensity as they had the other day in the mine shaft. *Oh, yes,* she thought, *it will indeed be terrible having him along.* How was she supposed to concentrate on searching for the mine when she'd forever be avoiding his all too intimate gaze?

Uncle Artemis had moved over to the survey the equipment and supplies. "Looks like everything I ordered is here. Good job, Cartier." Almost as an afterthought, he said, "Seeing as you two have already met, I don't suppose introductions are necessary."

"Yes, we have met," Edward said, his smile deepening. "Though it is a pleasure to make your acquaintance again, Mercy."

Mercy? Since when were they on a first name basis? If ever she needed the protection of formalities, it was now.

"If you'll excuse me, *Mr. Cartier*." She nodded and went to stand by her uncle, unnerved that Edward followed her.

Uncle Artemis and Frosty were examining a loose handle on a mallet.

"Shall I fetch Samson?" she asked.

"Good idea." Uncle Artemis handed the mallet back to Frosty. "Let's harness him up and see how he does around here. I won't have you taking him into those mountains if he trips in every pothole along the way. How's his hoof?"

"Much better. The farrier pronounced him 'sound' yesterday." For the last two weeks, Mercy had diligently treated the mule's hoof and pampered him to no end.

Uncle Artemis nodded. "That's good enough for me. Jake knows his business."

"Shall I help you with the mule?" Edward asked. "He can be quite stubborn."

"That's not necessary." She gathered her skirt around her and prepared for a hasty retreat. "I've been handling him without help for a while now. He's used to me."

"Stay here, Cartier, and give us a hand loading the equipment. Frosty's so slow, he'd lose a race with a sick snail."

For once, Mercy was grateful her uncle intervened. She hurried to the stock pen after retrieving a halter hanging on the hitching post. At the sound of the gate latch sliding, Samson's long ears twitched, and he lumbered over to investigate. He greeted her in his usual fashion, nosing her skirt pockets for an apple or other treat.

"Sorry, nothing today."

Samson expressed his disappointment by snorting.

Mercy slipped the halter over his head and buckled it, then she led him through the gate. He got around well for the most part, but this had become familiar ground in the past two weeks. What would he be like on the road with traffic coming and going? Or in the mountains on uneven terrain? After today, she'd have a better idea. Her grandfather's neighbor had once owned a blind horse who could plow a field straighter than any sighted horse. Were mules different than horses? A wave of anxiety stole Mercy's breath away. If Samson proved incapable of pulling a wagon, then once again her dream would be placed on indefinite hold.

"Just relax," she said and patted his neck. "You'll do fine."

At the stable, Samson stood quietly while being harnessed. Neither did he balk or fuss when Uncle Artemis and Edward hitched him to the wagon. With the last of the equipment and supplies loaded, they were ready for their trial run.

Uncle Artemis helped Mercy climb into the seat next to Edward. "It goes without saying that you're to bring my niece back safely."

Edward made sure the brake was set, then smiled affably. "Of course."

"I'm counting on you." A private look passed between the two men.

Mercy frowned. Something funny was going on with her uncle and Edward. She'd been told they'd reached an agreement. Edward was to watch over her, in return for some sort of monetary compensation. Yet, she couldn't dismiss the feeling that her uncle's warning contained an underlying message—one Edward obviously understood.

"Are you ready?" he asked, addressing her.

"Yes."

She gripped the side of the seat. The peculiar exchange between her uncle and Edward no longer mattered. What if

Samson bolted? What if he stumbled, or limped because his hoof hadn't healed properly? What if he ran the wagon off the road? A dozen disastrous possibilities flashed through her mind in a matter of seconds.

Edward released the brake, clucked to Samson, and snapped the reins. Uncle Artemis and Frosty, who'd been holding the mule's bridle, stood back, clear of harm's way. Mercy braced herself and waited for the wagon to lunge forward.

And waited. And waited.

Samson remained motionless.

Edward snapped the reins again. "Come along, *homme vieil*. What are you waiting for?"

The mule shook his head, then pawed the ground.

"I am impatient as well." Edward snapped the reins a third time. "Are you deaf as well as blind? Let us be off."

No amount of coaxing worked. Even Uncle Artemis slapping the mule on the hind quarters with his hat had no effect. Samson refused to budge.

Edward turned to Mercy. "Perhaps you should get down and whisper in his ear like you did at the mine."

"I don't think that's the problem."

"No?"

"The tunnels are narrow. He didn't have to see in order to pull the carts. Here in the open, it's different. It took me a full day to teach him how to find his way around the stock pen."

Edward shrugged, then grinned. "You may be right. He needs a teacher. Frosty," he called to the old prospector, "take your donkey and put her in front of the mule. See if he will follow her."

Frosty did as instructed. With a gentle tug on his bridle, Samson obediently followed the little donkey away from the stable and onto the main road.

Joy bubbled inside Mercy and without thinking, she laughed. At Edward's interested stare, she covered her mouth.

"Please. Do not stop. I like the sound of your laughter. You are much too serious, you know."

Was she? Mercy didn't think so. Something about Edward brought out her cautious side. Even now, sitting beside him, it took every ounce of her willpower not to press herself into the opposite end of the seat, putting as much space between them as possible.

"I don't mean to be so serious all the time, but finding the Silver Angel Mine is important to me."

"I heard about your father. Losing someone you love is difficult. You have my sympathies."

"Thank you." She hoped he wouldn't bring up the story of Buttercup carrying her dead father's body down the mountainside. If need be, she'd leap from the moving wagon before letting Edward see her cry. Fortunately, he didn't.

"Your father spent many years looking for the mine, did he not?"

"Yes, ten. He knew the *Mano del Diablo* Mountains better than anyone."

"Still, he never found the mine?"

"No." Mercy tried not to appear defensive. Nothing in Edward's tone indicated more than a casual interest. She told herself that questions were natural and to be expected. "But he might have, given more time."

Might have, if he hadn't fallen from a ledge and split his head open. Mercy pushed the uninvited thought of her father's prone and battered body to the back of her mind. She forced herself to remember him as he had been, a tall, vigorous man with an insatiable curiosity matched only by his zest for life.

"Time is not always kind to us."

Edward's remark gave Mercy pause. He spoke as if he

knew firsthand the pain of losing a loved one. Could it be? She peered at him from behind the brim of her straw hat, but his face showed no expression.

Samson pulled the wagon with ease, never falling more than two feet behind Buttercup's swishing tail. After several minutes of silence, Edward asked, "Have you decided where to begin your search?"

Shifting positions, Mercy discretely scratched an itch on the back of her neck. It was not yet eight o'clock in the morning, and already the sun beat down on them, hot and unrelenting. "The east rim of the third finger."

"Why there?"

"My father frequently mentions the east rim in his journal. He'd discovered several clues which all pointed to that location."

"He kept a journal? Interesting."

"It is. Very interesting." She warmed to the subject, momentarily forgetting her wariness of Edward. "I read it often, and I find something new each time."

Edward leaned forward, resting his forearms on his knees. "I would like very much to read this journal of your father's."

"No! What I mean is . . ." Mercy knew she had become overly attached to the journal, yet she couldn't bring herself to let it out of her possession. "The journal is one of the few possessions I have that belonged to my father. I wouldn't want anything to happen to it."

"I would be very careful."

She shook her head. "I can't take the chance. Despite our best intentions, things happen beyond our control."

He looked straight at her, his eyes searching her face as if he saw something there he didn't quite believe. "That is quite true."

For several long seconds, the world came to a standstill.

Then, abruptly, Edward turned away. Mercy blinked, slightly disoriented. What had just happened?

Drawing up on the reins, Edward pulled Samson to a stop. They'd reached the outskirts of the mining complex. "*Mon ami*," he called to Frosty. "Let us see how well the mule does without a teacher."

After tying Buttercup to the back of the wagon, Frosty climbed onto the seat beside Mercy. She was left with no choice but to scoot over next to Edward, so close their legs pressed together from hips to ankle. The temperature, suddenly and inexplicably, rose another fifteen degrees.

Samson did exceedingly well by himself, managing a tight turn without assistance.

"Look at that, will you." Forgetting her discomfort, Mercy clapped.

"It appears, *Mademoiselle*, you are officially in the prospecting business. When do we set out?"

"Set out?" Mercy's good cheer faded as reality sunk in. She'd been so busy worrying about Samson, she hadn't thought beyond their trial run around the mining complex. "I don't know."

"Why not today? It is Saturday, and we are not working."

"Today?"

"It is still early and the mountains are no more than an hour's drive from here."

"What about food? We'll need to eat."

Edward leaned forward and peered around Mercy. "Frosty, can you fix us some lunch buckets?"

"You betcha."

"We can't stay out late," Mercy said, chewing on a thumbnail. "I promised Aunt Connie I'd be up early and help her make pies for the company party tomorrow."

"Do not worry. We will go only for the day and be home

long before suppertime. Your uncle made it clear we were not to stay overnight."

"In that case, I suppose we could." Her hesitancy turned into excitement. "Yes. Why not?"

"It is agreed then." Edward beamed and clucked to Samson, urging the mule into a brisk trot. "We leave in search of the Silver Angel Mine."

Thunder cracked overhead at the same instant lightning split the late afternoon sky. When Mercy looked up, a fat raindrop landed squarely in one eye.

"Gosh darn it!"

She wiped at the raindrop, only to have a dozen more strike her straw hat with a soft pitter-patter. A few seconds later, the heavens opened wide and released a downpour, heralding the start of the monsoon season. Frosty had warned her the other day about the possibility of rain, and she'd chosen to ignore him.

"Edward!" she hollered. "Frosty!" Where had they gone off to? And why weren't they back yet?

She'd been left with the wagon and given strict orders not to go anywhere until the men returned, something she'd been more than happy to do.

Samson had done well earlier that morning on their five-mile drive to the *Mano del Diablo* Mountains. He'd pulled the heavy wagon over bumpy roads like a champion—until they'd reached the river. There, he'd refused to set one hoof in the water. They wasted a precious hour of daylight locating a place narrow enough and shallow enough to the mule's liking. Even then, they had to tie him to the back of Buttercup's pack saddle and lead him across.

Things didn't improve on the other side of the river.

Twice they got lost, disagreeing over the cryptic directions Mercy recalled from her father's journal. Edward had a surprise run-in with a cactus and came away with a leg full of stickers. Lastly, Mercy took a nasty tumble down a ravine, scraping her arms and tearing her skirt in the process. Edward had scolded at her, telling her to wear more appropriate footwear the next time. She stuck her tongue out at him. Frosty just laughed.

And if all that weren't enough, now they had the rain to contend with. She was already soaked to the skin.

Samson pawed the ground impatiently.

"I know, boy. They've been gone way too long for my peace of mind." She stood in the wagon, wrapped the reins around the brake handle, cupped her hands to her mouth, and hollered again. "Edward! Frosty! Where are you?"

To her vast relief, she heard a dim reply in the distance. A few minutes later, they emerged from a cluster of tall shrubs, wet, ragged, and dirty. Her heart leapt at the sight of them.

"You're back! Are you all right? Did you find the trail?"

While Frosty went to check on Buttercup, Edward climbed into the wagon with Mercy. "We followed it for almost half a mile before it came to a dead end on the other side of the ridge."

Mercy sighed.

"You could not expect us to find the mine . . . right out the gate, as you say."

"No." But neither had she expected them to meet with so many calamities on their first attempt.

"There is always next Saturday." He didn't strike her as being particularly distraught over their lack of luck.

Well, she couldn't blame him. His only stake in this venture was payment from her uncle. Unlike her, he didn't have a dream to fulfill and a father's reputation to save. Actually, from where she sat, Edward Cartier didn't appear to have a care in the world.

"Are you ready to go home?" Water soaked his shirt, turning it four shades darker.

"More than ready."

"So am I." He removed his hat and shook off the excess water before plunking it back on his head. "Frosty, make haste, *mon ami.*"

"*Oui, oui,*" Frosty said with a pronounced accent, hauling himself into the wagon next to Mercy. He gave her a toothless grin. "Edward's teachin' me to speak French."

"How lovely." She barely kept the sarcasm from her voice. "Shall we be off, gentlemen, before we drown?"

Less than a mile into their journey, they lost the trail and came face to face with a steep canyon wall. Edward turned Samson toward the river, but the mule had other ideas and balked once again. Their safe crossing place was a good thirty minutes in the opposite direction and with the storm showing no sign of letting up, none of them wished to backtrack.

"What's the problem?" Mercy shouted over the roar. As before, she'd been left alone in the wagon.

Edward stood in the river, knee-deep in the water and worn out from tugging on Samson's bridle. "Who knows," he shouted back. "The rain, the thunder and lightning, the sound of rushing water. He's frightened and confused."

He isn't the only one. Mercy looked back at Frosty, who was untying Buttercup from the wagon. "What are you doing?"

"This here girl ain't afraid. We're heading upriver a ways to see if there's a place to cross. If we don't find one soon, we'll be stuck here all night. And I for one don't want that."

"Frosty, I think we should stick together."

He walked up beside her, wiping the rain from his face with the back of his arm. "You got a better idea?"

She didn't. "Be careful. Please," she added softly.

"Take care," Edward said, clapping Frosty on the back.

"Nothing's gonna happen to me. It's her I'm worried about." He hitched a thumb at Mercy. "See she don't do nothing foolish."

"I am but one man." Edward grinned and held out both his hands in a gesture of surrender. "There is only so much I can do."

"Give it your best shot," Frosty said before leaving.

Samson brayed loudly at the loss of his little donkey friend.

"If you miss her so much, why do you not go after her?" Edward nudged the mule's hind quarters. He grunted, but otherwise stayed firmly in place. Edward then called the mule by his other name, the one the miners had given him.

Mercy gasped. "Well! I know you're frustrated, but was that really necessary?"

"Apparently not, for it had no effect."

"Maybe we should try to find some cover. There's a tall tree over there. We could pull the wagon under it."

Edward nodded. "It is as good a place as any to wait."

Turning Samson around, Mercy drove the wagon up the small embankment toward the tree. Edward brought up the rear on foot, giving the wagon an extra push when needed. Halfway there, he stopped, his gaze fixed on a not-too-distant hill. He didn't look happy.

Mercy drew up on the reins, halting Samson. "Is something wrong?"

"There is a rider on horseback. Can you see him?"

Lifting the brim of her hat, she squinted at the hill. "No, I don't."

"He was watching Frosty and I earlier when we were on the trail. I think he is following us."

"Following us? You can't be serious. Only an unbalanced person would be out in this rain." She quickly raised a finger. "And before you say anything, present company excluded."

"Go along," Edward motioned her ahead, "while I check on our visitor."

"You're not leaving too!"

"I will not be long."

"Edward, no. What if the man's dangerous? You think you can march right up to him and demand an explanation?"

"Of course not. I will double back the way we came and surprise him from behind."

Mercy bolted to her feet, gripped by sudden fear. "What if he means to harm us? He could have a gun. These mountains are full of bootleggers and their secret lairs. They shoot first and ask questions later."

"I am touched by your concern." His amused smile reached all the way to his eyes. "I had begun to think you did not like me."

"This isn't a joke."

"I am capable of protecting myself if the need arises."

Did he think himself invincible? "With what? Your pocket comb?"

"No, *chère*." He reached down and pulled something from his boot. "With this."

Lightning flashed, and Mercy saw he held a knife, the steel blade glinting as he skillfully danced it between his fingers.

"Where did you get that?" she asked in a hoarse voice.

"I am never without it." Flicking his wrist, he twirled the knife and replaced it in his boot. "As you can see, I am something of an expert."

"Yes . . . you are."

With a start, Mercy realized she'd been too quick in dismissing the majority of rumors surrounding Edward. He handled a six-inch steel blade as if it were a teaspoon, and that made him a dangerous man.

* * *

The flame inside the glass globe flickered weakly. Mercy carefully adjusted the knob on the lantern's base and when the flame suddenly caught and grew, she sighed with relief. It had taken her twenty minutes of rifling through the wagon bed in the dark to find the can of kerosene and a dry match, but the rewards were worth it. She had light!

Walking around the wagon, she returned to her place under the tree's protective limbs. There, she hung the lantern on a low branch and sat on the damp ground next to where Samson was tied. Within minutes, several dozen flying insects collected around the lantern, beating the glass globe with their tiny wings.

Mercy peered at the sky through the branches. The rain had quit as abruptly as it had begun, leaving behind a thick cloud which blocked the stars and moon. Hugging herself, she shivered. It was surprisingly chilly. Her clothes clung to her, stiff and scratchy.

A pack of coyotes howled nearby and Mercy shivered again, this time from fright. It hadn't taken the nocturnal creatures of the desert long to come out of hiding after the storm abated. At every screech, squawk, and rustle, she jumped—which, in turn, spooked Samson.

She didn't know how long she'd been waiting. Cold, hunger, exhaustion, and fear hampered her ability to think clearly. If Edward or Frosty didn't return soon, she was heading for home without them. By her calculations, Paradise couldn't be more than four miles away. She'd walked that distance before and would gladly do it again if it meant a hot bath and the comfort of her own bed.

Of course, those other four-mile walks had been through the streets of Boston in broad daylight—not in the desert, late at night, with a strange man on horseback possibly stalking her.

At a loud, whirring noise behind her, Mercy stood and

darted out from under the tree, instinctively covering her head with her arms. She let out a yelp as what seemed like a thousand bats surrounded her. They came so close she could feel the wind generated by their flapping wings. Their high-pitched squeaks filled her ears until she thought she'd scream. Then a tiny claw brushed her cheek.

Panic consumed her and without thinking, she ran.

Stumbling down the embankment, she reached the river and, unable to stop her momentum, fell in. The frigid water shocked her, as did the strong current, which pulled at her with alarming force. Struggling to stand, she slid on a slimy rock and lost her footing. The scream she'd been holding back tore from her throat, then died as her head went under water.

She came up sputtering and gasping for air, her heart beating so hard it hurt. The current was carrying her swiftly down the river. Her shoes skittered over the rocky bottom, unable to find solid footing. Her clothes, heavier wet than dry, dragged her under. Arms thrashing and legs kicking, she tried her best to stay afloat.

Oh, dear God, am I going to die?

She must get to shore. It wasn't far. She could make it.

Sucking in a fortifying breath, she pushed with her feet and propelled herself toward shore. Just as she thought she might make it, she crashed into a huge boulder sticking up out of the water. Pain radiated through her shoulders and back, robbing her of what little strength she had left.

It was all she could do to keep her head above water.

Then, even that small effort became too much.

All at once, strong arms grabbed her and hauled her from the water. She felt herself being lifted and carried—by whom, she didn't know or care. What mattered most was that the river hadn't swallowed her.

"Thank you," she whispered, her head drooping onto her chest.

"I should wring your neck for what you did."

"Edward?" she murmured. "Is that you?"

"Yes." He sounded angry.

"Are you mad at me?"

"You almost drowned."

"I'm sorry." They reached the bank, and he set her down. Mercy's wobbly legs weren't able to support her, and she slumped to the ground, taking Edward with her. "I got scared. There were all these bats. Hundreds of them. They attacked me."

"The bats around here don't attack people. They eat nectar or insects. Like birds."

"Insects?" Mercy thought of the lantern and the multitude of winged insects attracted to it. That did explain the appearance of the bats. Still, his condescending attitude annoyed her. She'd practically died, for crying out loud! "How am I supposed to know what bats eat?" Anger revived her, and she managed to sit up. "I'm from Boston."

"Exactly," he growled. "What do you know about the desert and mountains? If I had not returned when I did, the fish would be dining on you for breakfast."

"You shouldn't have left me alone." She pushed at him, angry tears spilling from her eyes.

"You should have stayed with the wagon like I told you to." He gripped her firmly with his hands and pulled her to him. His dark eyes glinted as brightly as the steel blade of his knife had earlier. "Promise me you will never do anything stupid like that again."

His tight hold caused her sore shoulders to ache, but she didn't care. She was too lost in his mesmerizing gaze for anything else to register. "I wish I could, but I can't. I've always been a little headstrong."

"I have noticed that about you," he said in a softer voice. Letting go with one hand, he tenderly brushed a wet strand of hair from her face. "It is an irritating habit." His mouth moved closer and closer to hers. "If we are to continue being partners, you will have to start listening to me."

"That won't be easy."

"Try."

He uttered the last word against her lips.

In the next instant, Mercy knew what it was like to be kissed by a man. Really, truly, and thoroughly kissed.

Chapter Four

March 27, 1909

*B*roke *my thumb today when a boulder we were moving rolled on it. Won't be making many journal entries
the next few weeks. Frosty fashioned a splint out of twigs
and twine. He's taking me to Paradise tomorrow so the
doctor can set the bone. He also forced me to drink some
rank tea that's supposed to help with the pain.*

It doesn't work.

*Going to bed as soon as I write Mercy a letter.
Promised her I'd send one every month. It will be short,
though. This blasted thumb hurts too much.*

Charles Oliver Bidwell

"Would you like some coffee?"

Edward looked up from where he sat on a dainty and
remarkably uncomfortable chair in the Bidwell's front parlor. Connie Bidwell held a china cup out to him, which he
gratefully accepted.

It had been a long day and, by the sound of all the shouting coming from the kitchen, it was far from over. Artemis Bidwell had a lot to say to his niece. At the rate he was going, they'd be lucky to get to bed by midnight.

Taking a sip of the rich brew, Edward nodded at Mrs. Bidwell. "This is good. Thank you."

"We should be thanking you, Mr. Cartier, for rescuing our niece." The plump, pleasant-looking woman assessed him critically from her higher vantage point. "My husband was right to hire you. I admit I wasn't sold on the idea at first. Please don't take offense, but the rumors circulating about you are a bit disconcerting."

"No offense taken." He took another sip of coffee, hiding his smile in the china cup.

"But you've proved my doubts wrong, and surpassed both Mr. Bidwell's and my expectations. I can rest easier knowing Mercy will be in your capable hands the next time she goes gallivanting into those ghastly mountains."

"You think there will be a next time?" Edward cast a sideways glance at the door leading to the kitchen. The echo of Artemis Bidwell's angry pacing reverberated throughout the entire house.

Mrs. Bidwell raised her brows and said evenly, "You don't know my niece very well if you think there won't be a next time."

No, he didn't know Mercy well, but what he did know might shock Mrs. Bidwell and destroy the confidence she had in him.

He knew the taste and texture of Mercy's sweet lips, which he'd learned during the many kisses they'd shared before Frosty stumbled upon them. He also knew the shape of her soft, womanly form—how it fit perfectly in his arms. He also knew the scent of her skin, having discovered it when he buried his face in her neck rather than tempt himself past the point of no return.

Kissing her had been an impulse. He certainly hadn't planned on it when he saw her floating down the river, floundering at first and then going still. He'd been afraid in that instant, more afraid than he could ever remember being. His relief at pulling her from the river, alive and unharmed, had been overwhelming and disturbing. Why should he care what happened to her? She was a means to an end, an opportunity to earn a bonus and help his family survive another winter—nothing more.

Then he'd kissed her, and she'd kissed him back. Edward realized he was beginning to care for her more than he should—more than was safe, or wise, or fitting.

Guilt ate a hole in his stomach worse than a shot of bad whiskey. Mrs. Bidwell was wrong to place her confidence in him. The chances were a hundred times more likely Mercy would be hurt by him than some disaster encountered during her hunt for the mine. He could almost guarantee it. The last thing Edward wanted or needed was to become involved with another woman—not when he had yet to get over the last one.

"Would you care for a bite of supper?" Mrs. Bidwell asked, changing the subject.

"That would be nice."

"There isn't much, mind you, cold chicken and leftover cornbread is all."

"A feast to a starving man such as myself." He was, in fact, so hungry he could probably eat the lace doily on the little table beside him if she poured honey over it.

She dismissed his compliment with a wave and a laugh. "Sara Jane Ketchem was right. You *are* a smooth talker. Supper won't take me more than a few minutes," she said over her shoulder as she toddled toward the kitchen. "I'll call when it's ready."

Alone, Edward stood and stretched, glad tomorrow was

Sunday, the day of rest. Walking off the kinks in his legs
caused by the uncomfortable chair, he strolled to the fireplace
mantle, where he studied a row of silver-framed photographs.

In the first one, a much younger Artemis Bidwell, dressed
in a short-sleeved shirt and work pants and holding a shovel, stood in front of a hole in the mountain. A rickety shack
sat off to the side. This rustic setting, Edward guessed, was
the entrance to the main tunnel, many years before in the
early days of the Paradise Consolidated Copper Company.

The next picture, considerably newer, showed two men in
front of mining headquarters. They were both smiling, the
hand of one resting affectionately on the shoulder of the
other. They looked too much alike not to be brothers.

That assumption was confirmed at the end of the mantle,
after a half-dozen pictures of Artemis Bidwell, his wife, and
three sons in various stages of their lives. There, Edward
found and picked up a family portrait of Mercy and her parents, the man obviously the same one as in the earlier picture with Artemis Bidwell.

A child version of Mercy sat primly between her parents,
her stockinged legs and polished black shoes sticking out
from under a checkered dress which barely covered her
knees. Hands folded in her lap, she strived for the appearance of a perfect young lady. The large, crooked bow on the
top of her head and the elfish gleam in her eyes, however,
gave away her true nature. Her parents weren't smiling, as
was the custom in portraits, yet something in their expres-
sions radiated contentment. *And love*, Edward thought,
replacing the picture on the mantle.

He considered his immediate family, all twelve of them.
Mercy was the only one left a7live in hers. How would he
feel in the same situation, as the sole surviving member of a
once happy family? He might know soon enough if condi-
tions at home didn't improve. The Cartiers faced another

long, cold winter with an empty storehouse and an even emptier cash box.

No! He wouldn't let them perish. Whatever it took, whatever the cost, he would safeguard them, even if it meant compromising his integrity—something, despite rumors to the contrary, he didn't do.

"Come and get it," Connie Bidwell called from the kitchen.

Edward waited in the doorway for a signal to enter. If he hadn't already accepted Mrs. Bidwell's offer, he might have turned around and left. The tension in the otherwise cozy room was so thick, a person would have to be unconscious not to sense it.

"Make yourself at home," chirped Mrs. Bidwell, setting a wicker basket covered with a cloth in the center of a sturdy pine table.

Mercy sat at the table, her gaze on her lap. Her uncle sat beside her, looking like he was ready to throttle somebody. Edward took the empty chair across from him, hoping it placed him out of arm's reach.

"I'd like to thank you, Cartier, for what you did tonight." Artemis Bidwell acknowledged Edward with a curt nod. "No telling what would have happened to Mercy if you hadn't been there to save her."

"No thanks are necessary," Edward replied with uncharacteristic solemnity. He didn't think it wise to make too much of the rescue. His instincts proved accurate as, in the next instant, he became the target of his boss' wrath.

"Of course, she wouldn't have jumped in the river in the first place if you hadn't left her. I hired you to protect her."

"Yes, sir."

"I took it for granted you understood what that entailed. To stay with her at all times."

"It is my fault. I should not have left her alone for any reason. You are right to be angry with me."

Mercy's head shot up, and she gave him a confused look.

"Darn tootin' it's your fault!" Artemis Bidwell slapped the table with the flat of his hand. "However, if my niece here had followed orders for once in her life . . ." He let the sentence dangle.

"Rest assured, I will not make the same mistake in the future." Edward didn't touch the plate of cold chicken Mrs. Bidwell placed in front of him.

"Don't trouble yourself about it. There won't be a next time."

"Uncle Artemis!" Mercy came off her chair, then sat back down when her aunt put a restraining hand on her. "You promised me."

"That was before you almost killed yourself."

"It was an accident." Her gaze shot to Edward, then back to her uncle. "I swear from now on I'll follow Mr. Cartier's orders to the letter."

"I said *no*." He stood and leveled a finger at her. "You are not to set foot within a mile of those mountains again. Do you hear me, Mercy?"

"You can't tell me what to do." Mercy's voice quavered with suppressed emotion. "You're not my father."

For a moment, Artemis Bidwell's jaw went slack and his eyes clouded with pain. Then he slowly pushed in his chair, using the excuse to collect himself. "No one can replace your father and it may be wrong of me to try, but I love you like you were my own daughter, Mercy, and only want what's best for you."

"I'm sorry, Uncle," she said contritely, lifting her face to his. "I didn't mean that the way it came out."

Edward felt like an intruder. "I should be leaving. Thank you, Mrs. Bidwell, for the supper."

"You haven't touched a bite," she chided. Taking charge of the situation, she expertly defused it with a skill undoubtedly learned from many years of marriage. "Come along, Artemis, and leave these two young people alone to finish eating." She tugged on his arm. "Everything's been said that needs to be said, and then some. A good night's sleep will do us all a world of good."

He hesitated briefly before relenting. "You're right. There's no need to involve Cartier more than we already have. We'll take this up in the morning when we're rested. Good night." He turned and followed his wife.

Edward had always respected the mine superintendent, but never more than he did at that moment. They were a lot alike in many ways. They both knew when to step down from a fight, and they both put the welfare of their children ahead of their own.

"Well," Mercy gave Edward a weak smile once they were alone, "I'm glad that's finally over." She pushed the basket containing the cornbread toward him. "Go on and eat. You don't want to insult my aunt."

"What about you?"

"I'm not very hungry."

She looked so miserable, Edward made an attempt to console her. "That is the bad thing about words. You cannot take them back once they are said."

Her eyes blazed. "I don't need a lecture from you, too."

So much for consoling her. Maybe now she'd eat. "I apologize. It was not my intention to lecture you. I had thought to cheer you."

Mercy picked at her chicken. "Why did you take the blame for what happened?"

"Why wouldn't I?"

"I'm the one who ran off."

"Yes, but your uncle hired me to take care of you."

Her mouth turned down at the corners. "We shouldn't have involved you in our family dispute."

"Do not worry." Edward made quick work of a chicken leg. Having started eating, he couldn't stop. "I am from a large family. I am used to disputes."

She brightened. "Really? How large?"

"I have two brothers and seven sisters."

"Oh, my goodness!" Mercy pressed a hand to her throat.

"That surprises you?"

"I guess it does. I thought of you more as a loner."

"I am alone now."

"So am I." She resumed picking at her chicken.

Edward buttered a second piece of cornbread. "You have your uncle and his family."

"It's not the same." She sighed wistfully.

"They care for you very much."

"I know, and I don't want to hurt them, but Uncle Artemis is so strict." Mercy started to say more, then clamped her mouth shut. "Let's talk about something else. Do you visit your family often?"

"I have not seen them since I left Canada two years ago."

"How sad. You must miss them." She'd finally begun to eat, taking small bites of food and sipping on her coffee.

A wave of acute homesickness washed over Edward. "Yes, very much." At her dubious expression, he asked, "You do not believe me?"

"I do. It's just that . . ." She laughed nervously. "You must know that people here talk about you, and nothing they say paints you as a family man."

"What do they say? Tell me," he coaxed when she shook her head.

"They say . . . they say . . ." Mercy gulped. "They say you are a ladies' man."

"Ah." Amused, Edward sat back and rubbed his chin.

"You don't deny it?"

He did, but the temptation to tease Mercy was always too

great to resist. "That might be difficult after what happened tonight when I pulled you from the river."

Her cheeks burned a bright red. She fussed with her disheveled hair, then asked almost shyly, "Is it true you left Canada because of a woman?"

"That particular rumor is true." He became suddenly quiet, his mind and heart turning inward. "I did leave because of a woman. Actually, a girl. Her name is Jacqueline."

His honesty clearly shocked Mercy. She didn't immediately respond and, when she did, it was in a whisper. "Jacqueline is your wife?"

"No. My wife is dead." Edward met Mercy's wide-eyed stare. "Jacqueline is my daughter."

Mercy's fork clattered to the table, and she quickly snatched it up.

His daughter!

She didn't know whether to be relieved or upset, eventually settling on the former. After all, she and Edward had kissed a few hours ago, and it wouldn't do if he turned out to be married.

A daughter.

Never in a thousand years would she have suspected him of being a father, a father who'd left his daughter behind— just like her father had left her behind in boarding school.

She stiffened at the realization. To think she'd imagined herself attracted to a man like him. Poor little Jacqueline. First her mother died, and then her father went away. Mercy knew exactly how the girl felt.

"You are irritated with me." He correctly read her mood change.

"It's not my place to judge other people," she answered primly.

"Yet you do it," his expression was mildly accusing, "and

without knowing all the facts. Does it bother you that I was once married?"

"Hardly."

"That I have a daughter?"

"Of course not!"

"What then?"

She allowed her jumbled emotions to get the better of her and exclaimed, "What kind of father abandons his only child?"

Edward went utterly still, and a dark shadow passed over his face. "I did not abandon my child." He rose forcefully to his feet, his chair making an awful sound as its legs scraped across the wooden floor. "She is everything in the world to me."

His words, so full of anger and misery, came at her like tiny bullets. She involuntarily flinched. "It's not—"

He didn't let her finish. "I left because I had no choice. It was either that, or stay and watch Jacqueline die, along with the rest of my family."

Mercy's anger instantly evaporated. "Die? How?" Her questions were uttered on a thin puff of air.

"From starvation." Replacing the chair, he took his leave. "Please thank your aunt for me."

After a moment's indecision, she chased after him, catching up with him at the front door, where he was collecting his hat from a hook on the wall.

She took his arm and waylaid him before he could step outside. "I jumped to a conclusion. Convince me it's the wrong one."

He looked down at her hand resting in the crook of his elbow, then back up at her. "I do not owe you, or anyone, an explanation."

"That's true, but I want to know. I . . . need to know. Please."

"Why?"

"It's difficult to explain."

"Convince me," he said in a mocking tone.

She released his arm, her hand dropping to her side. It was hard. The pain was still there, buried deep inside her, even after all these years. She swallowed in an effort to overcome it.

"I was twelve-years-old when my mother died of a fever. My father, quite simply, fell apart. He and my mother were very much in love, you see."

Mercy waited for Edward to comment. When he didn't, she continued with her story. "After a time, he enrolled me in boarding school and traveled the country, eventually settling in Paradise. I never really understood why he left. I suppose he didn't know how to comfort a miserable and lonely little girl who missed her mother. He incorrectly assumed that the guidance of women instructors and the companionship of other girls would help." Mercy's throat closed at the rush of unhappy memories. She risked a glance at Edward. There was compassion in his expression, not the disinterest or scorn she'd expected.

"Go on," he said gently.

Mercy continued, though she'd never discussed her father with anyone—not even Uncle Artemis or Frosty. "He wrote me every month, and I saved each of his letters, reading them over and over until the pages were worn through in places. They were the only bright spot in an otherwise dull life."

"I find that hard to believe. Boston is a large city."

"Yes, but the Boston Academy for Young Women is very conservative. I was allowed few privileges, and that didn't change after I graduated and began working in their office. I was expected—no, required—to set an example for the female students attending the academy. I dreamed day and night of coming here to join my father in his quest for the Silver Angel Mine."

She sighed and swallowed again. "I hoarded every spare penny I earned until I had enough money for train passage, but I never saw my father again. He died two weeks before I arrived." She studied Edward's face, seeking the answers her father had failed to provide in any of his many letters. "Why would a parent leave their only child? What possible reason is more important than them?"

"I cannot speak for your father. I can only tell you that if he loved you as much as I love Jacqueline, the decision to leave was not an easy one."

"Then why do it?"

"I told you."

"You told me your family was starving, but it sounds to me like you left to save yourself."

He turned on her, the cold edge from earlier returning in a flash. "Nothing in this world is more important to me than my family. If need be, I would sell my soul to the devil to save them." His eyes were like two slits of black jet. "Sometimes I think I already have."

Every nerve in Mercy's body urged her to back away. She didn't, however, and remained in place, though beneath her skirt, her legs wobbled. "Why?"

Edward stared at her a moment longer, then shook his head. His face was empty of expression. "It does not matter," he said, opening the door and stepping out onto the porch.

Mercy blocked his leaving again. She scooted around him and placed herself directly in his path. "Tell me about them. Tell me about your family." Her desperate need to know pulled at her, twisting her middle into a tight coil. Perhaps Edward could tell her something that would help her to understand her father, and forgive him for the hurt and misery he'd caused her.

In the square of pale yellow light coming from the parlor window, she saw Edward tense. A soft breeze drifted onto the porch, ruffling his hair and the folds of his soiled work shirt. Nothing else about him moved. For a moment, she was certain he'd refuse her request and brush by her. Then, staring at a distant point in the darkness beyond, he began talking.

"We are farmers. For five generations, the Cartiers have raised crops and livestock on the same hundred acres in a small town outside of Montreal. Then three years ago, we suffered the worst drought in history. All the crops failed and soon after that, the lambs began dying. We sold the pigs to make it through the first winter. After that, we had nothing. When spring came, we needed money for food and seed and breeding stock. There was no work in town, so I left to find what I could. A foreman's job pays well. I send most of my wages home to my family."

"Why you?"

"I am the logical choice."

"How so? You mentioned brothers and sisters."

"Two of my sisters are married and living with their husbands. My unmarried sisters embroider and sell what they can at the local market, which is not much. My brother, Jean, is only twelve and too young to find decent-paying work. Besides, he must help with the farm. My father is sick with rheumatism. He and my mother could not manage without Jean."

"What about your other brother? Is he also married?"

"No."

Mercy thought only of the orphaned Jacqueline when she asked, "Why can't he be the one to leave?"

"Because he is a priest," Edward said matter-of-factly. "I am responsible for our family. He is responsible for the entire town."

"Oh." She bit her bottom lip, chagrined at her outspokenness.

"I have not seen my daughter in two years." His jaw flexed, the sole visible sign of his inner turmoil. "She is four now, and lives with one of my married sisters and her family. Sometimes I wonder if she remembers me."

"I'm sure she does."

The timbre in Edward's voice had changed, and the long-ing in it affected Mercy. Had her father wondered the same thing about her?

"You could return home for a visit," she suggested.

"When I return home, it will be for good." His gaze fell on her, where it stayed, unwavering. "I will not be separated from Jacqueline again."

Mercy resisted the temptation to wilt under his intimidat-ing stare. "For her sake, I hope that's true."

Something in Edward's eyes shifted. "I am sorry your father disappointed you, but I am not like him." He placed his hat on his head, indicating their conversation had reached its conclusion. "That is a promise."

He took the porch steps in one leap and crossed the small yard to the front gate. Opening it, he let himself out and headed down the street, presumably to where he lived in the company-provided housing on the opposite end of town.

Mercy stayed and watched until the black night swal-lowed the last trace of him, after which she went back inside and climbed the stairs to her small room on the second floor.

As she dressed for bed, she thought about Edward. More than anything, she wanted to believe him. Believe that, unlike her father, he wouldn't forever abandon his daughter to the care of others. His reasons for leaving Canada and his family made sense. Some would even call them commend-able. Yet her heart had trouble accepting them.

Then again, when it came to Edward Cartier, her heart had all manner of trouble.

Chapter Five

Though his offer of assistance appears genuine enough, I don't trust young Mr. Houseman. Having grown up in the area, he's familiar with the country-side and local folklore, some of which he imparted to us this evening around the campfire. But the fanatical gleam in his eyes disturbs me, enough so I remain cautious in my dealings with him.

He wants to join our expedition. In exchange, he will act as guide and share his vast knowledge of the mine, which could greatly aid our search. As he talked, I found myself absently fingering the silver ring. I couldn't help thinking of his father, the rancher from whom I purchased it. The two look nothing alike and are of completely different minds. The senior Mr. Houseman is a gentleman and, despite disbelieving in the existence of the Silver Angel Mine, an intellect.

His son is also intelligent, but more cunning, and, I

*fear, more dangerous. I've spent the last hour trying to
convince myself to accept his proposition and have had
no success. If ever I met a man with a hidden agenda,
it is him.*

                                    Charles Oliver Bidwell.

The lively strum of banjo music floated on the breeze to
where Edward sat with a group of miners behind the warehouse. Using blocks of wood or overturned buckets for
seats, they formed a close circle beneath the shade of a large
Palo Verde tree. There, removed from view, they passed the
time observing the flurry of activity in the open area in front
of mining headquarters.

Women in their Sunday finery scurried to and fro, laying
out dishes of food on long, cloth covered tables. Workers set
up chairs and benches around a makeshift dance floor. On a
raised stand next to the dance floor, musicians tuned their
instruments. At their feet, young children played tag and
jump rope. At the center of it all stood Connie Bidwell, magically creating order from chaos.

Every year, on the first Sunday in August, the Paradise
Consolidated Copper Company gave a huge party for the
employees and their families. And every year Connie Bidwell
organized the event, which always came off without a hitch.

By informal agreement, Edward's crew, themselves
recently bathed and sporting clean clothes, met under the tree
to relax and share a drink before the party started. When one
of the flasks being passed from hand to hand reached Edward,
he declined. That triggered several comments from the men.

"What's the matter, Cartier?" Mort Carmichael asked,
smacking his lips with appreciation after partaking a healthy
swig from his own flask. "You ain't one to thumb your nose
at a shot of corn whiskey, especially if it's free."

Edward ignored the dig, as he had all the others. Ever since the day they'd brought the old mule up from the mine, the surly engineer hadn't missed an opportunity to beleaguer Edward in public—or private, for that matter.

"I bet I know why he's not drinking," said Mort, a snide grin splitting his homely face. "Heard tell you was out late yesterday night with the boss's niece."

A chorus of raucous laughter and elbowing followed.

"Enough," Edward barked. He wouldn't allow anyone to malign Mercy. The men, used to following his orders, fell silent.

His gaze automatically wandered to the crowd, searching for her. She was easy to spot. Her outfit, like most of her clothes, was distinctly different in style and color from those of the other women. Most notable was the length of her skirt, which came to the tops of her ankles. While those lovely ankles were modestly covered by a pair of dark stockings, they still captured the attention of every male there—Edward included.

He wasn't sure where they stood after last night. Kissing her had been a mistake, compounded by their later argument. He'd been furious—but at himself, not her. Hardly a day passed that Edward didn't feel guilty about leaving Jacqueline behind. Mercy simply had the misfortune of bringing that guilt to the surface, at a time when he was already grappling with his attraction to her and where it might lead.

On the walk home from her uncle's house, he'd tried to convince himself it was best to have nothing to do with Mercy other than work—and he'd succeeded, for a few hours.

Seeing her this afternoon, looking the way she did, he realized he wanted to kiss her again.

Probably not one of his better ideas.

"She's a pretty one," an old-timer chimed in, "but if you

ask me, she ain't got the sense God gave a flea. What kind of girl goes traipsing off into the mountains looking for a mine?"

"Like father, like daughter." Mort snorted derisively and took another swallow from his flask. "Both of them are cracked in the head."

"I would watch how I talk about the young lady if I were you." Edward didn't have to raise his voice.

The group became instantly quiet. Every head turned in Mort's direction, awaiting his response.

"Oh." His eyes widened in mock fear. "Is that a threat?"

Edward tried to check the anger building inside him. It wasn't easy. "Insult me if you wish, but not her."

Mort's grin turned snide. "You wanna make something of it?"

Guillermo, who sat beside Edward, nudged him lightly in the arm. "Go on, *amigo*. You can beat him."

The idea was tempting, and Edward considered it. As much as he wanted to put the other man in his place—preferably with a right uppercut to the chin—he resisted. There was nothing to be gained, and much to lose; most significantly, his job. With hundreds of men working together, disagreements were inevitable. In order to maintain control, rules were strictly enforced. And fighting was against the rules. More than one miner had joined the ranks of the unemployed for taking a swing at a coworker.

Eventually, and probably soon, Mort would go too far, leaving Edward no choice but to resolve the situation as he saw fit. However, he'd rather it be a time and place of his choosing, and on his terms—not Mort's.

"Yeah, go on," a man on the other side of the circle said with a crude chuckle, encouraging the men to fight. "You'd be doing us all a favor."

"There's more than enough of this to go around." Mort

held up a clenched fist, his expression vile. "I can take on both of you with one had tied behind my back."

"I'd pay to see that," another man roared, slapping his thigh.

"You'd have to." The old-timer banged his pipe on the side of his boot, knocking loose the ash. "That's the only way Carmichael here will fight anyone."

Mort jumped up and tossed his flask onto the ground. He charged across the circle to stand in front of Edward. Feet spread and hands on hips, he jerked his head to one side, issuing a challenge. "Let's see what you're made of, Cartier."

Edward stood, hoping his greater height would intimidate the shorter man into backing down. It didn't work, though Mort hesitated momentarily.

"Don't tell me you're afraid to fight." He jabbed Edward in the chest with his index finger. "I reckon all those stories about you and the Riverside Gang aren't true."

The taunt was intended to incite Edward into throwing the first punch. That way, Mort could claim self-defense and save his job. It took every ounce of Edward's willpower not to rise to the bait.

Gloating, Mort surveyed the group. "Well, boys, looks like we finally know the truth. Cartier's plumb scared." He squawked and flapped his arms in imitation of a chicken, then dissolved into laughter at his own joke.

The laughter died in his throat when Edward grabbed him by the shirt front and lifted him into the air with one hand until their eyes were level.

"Shut up, Carmichael."

"Put me down," the engineer rasped, clawing uselessly at Edward's hand.

They stayed in that position for several seconds. No one in the group moved as Edward's grip tightened. Eventually, Mort started wheezing.

Suddenly Thomas stepped between them. Laying a hand on each of their shoulders, he pried them apart. "Here now, what's the use of fighting? The party'll be starting soon, and you don't want to scare off them ladies with your black eyes and busted lips."

The advice was good, and Edward heeded it for many reasons, one being his snap decision to ask Mercy to dance. He released his hold, and Mort dropped to his knees, gasping for breath.

Clapping Thomas on the back, Edward said, "You are right, *mon ami*." He then reached out a hand to Mort. "Let me help you."

"I don't need your help, Frenchman." Mort slapped Edward's hand away. He clambered to his feet unassisted and retrieved his flask from where it had fallen. Rounding on Edward, he growled, "We ain't through with this. Not by a long shot." He then pushed his way between two of the seated men and disappeared into the crowd.

"I think he's serious," Thomas commented dryly to Edward.

"I believe you are right."

"Good riddance," someone muttered loudly as Edward and Thomas settled into their seats.

Conversation resumed, and continued until a bell rang, signaling the start of supper. One by one the men got up, stretched, tucked in their shirts, and rambled toward the gathering.

Edward held back. He didn't want anyone with him when he asked Mercy to dance. Wrong as it may be, he was bound and determined to hold her in his arms again. Dancing presented the quickest and most socially acceptable method.

Thomas and Guillermo apparently had other plans. They fell into step beside Edward, one on either side.

"I am very hungry, *amigo*. What about you?" The young

Mexican raised his head and sniffed the air. He was not as tall as Edward, but built like an ox and just as strong. "Something smells *muy delicioso.*"

"I am not hungry." Edward attempted to rid himself of his friends without appearing rude. "Perhaps I will skip supper."

"Don't let that stunt Carmichael pulled ruin a good time." Thomas, never one to rile easily, dismissed the engineer.

Edward didn't respond. He let his friends assume the confrontation with Mort was the reason for his loss of appetite.

"He is a small man here," Guillermo said, tapping his head. "And here," he continued, tapping the place over his heart.

They all laughed. And because he wound up staying with his friends, Edward was soon stuck in the middle of the food line, surrounded by people. Unless he preferred having two dozen witnesses, asking Mercy to dance would have to wait.

The line moved intolerably slow. At each table, more and more food was piled onto their plates. Shredded beef, ham steaks, beans, cabbage, corn on the cob, fluffy white biscuits, and thick slices of bright red watermelon.

At the last table Mercy served generous portions of pie. She wore an exceedingly large hat adorned with multicolored feathers and artificial flowers. On another woman, it might have looked ridiculous, but not Mercy. Smiling and chatting with every person who stopped for pie, she made an engaging picture. Edward couldn't take his eyes off her.

"Hey, get a move on," came a gruff voice from behind.

"Sorry." He didn't realize he'd been holding up the line.

The next minute found him standing in front of her. She was even more dazzling up close, and he completely forgot the presence of his friends.

"Cherry, peach, or mincemeat?" She looked up, and the smile on her face froze.

He'd have to remedy that. "Did you make these pies?"

"Some . . . yes."

"Which ones?"

"The, um, peach pie is one of mine."

"Peach is my favorite." Edward made a show of examining the pie. "But the crust is a little burned on the edges."

"Burned? Where? I don't see any burned places."

"There." Edward indicated a teeny, tiny dark speck.

"That's not burned."

"If you say so." He shrugged.

She opened her mouth to speak, then snapped it shut. "You're teasing me."

"A little." He employed his most winning smile. "Will you dance with me later?"

Her cheeks bloomed pink. "I—I . . ."

"Oh, for pity's sake," grumbled the voice behind Edward. "Quit dawdling and tell the man yes. Some of us want to eat."

Edward and Mercy exchanged amused grins, the tension between them melting.

As he held out his plate to receive his peach pie, Edward caught a flash of movement in his peripheral vision. He looked down in time to see a small, grubby hand reach out from underneath the table, snatch a whole pie, and disappear.

"What the . . ."

Setting his plate down, he lifted the tablecloth, reached underneath, and hauled out the thief—all eighty pounds of him.

Mercy gasped. "What in the world is going on?"

Edward had just set the boy on his feet when he made a run for it. He didn't get two feet before Edward nabbed him by the shirt collar and jerked him back. Then he walked the boy away from the line of people and out of the way.

"Let me go!" He thrashed and kicked like someone possessed.

"Don't hurt him," Mercy cried, darting out from behind the table. "He's just a child."

"Hurt *him*?" Edward ducked as a flying fist almost struck him in the nose. "What about me?"

Thomas sauntered over to stand beside Edward. "At the rate he's going, he'll tire out soon. Can you last that long, or do you need me to relieve you for a spell?"

"I think I can manage."

"*Sí*," Guillermo said, joining them. "If he can handle Carmichael, he can surely handle one skinny little boy."

"Handle Carmichael?" Mercy stared curiously at Edward. "What's that all about?"

"Nothing." Edward shook his head. "A joke is all."

"Appears he's losing steam." Thomas swiped at the watermelon juice running down his chin with the cuff of his sleeve.

"Be careful," Guillermo warned. "It might be a trick."

Mercy heaved an impatient sigh. "Let him go, Edward. He obviously doesn't have the strength to walk from here to the next table." The boy had quit struggling and slumped over.

Not yet trusting his prisoner, Edward supported him by both shoulders and leaned down. "What is your name, son?"

The boy closed his mouth, refusing to answer.

Edward could feel the sharp edge of bones underneath the tattered clothes the boy wore, and scratches covered every inch of his exposed skin. Huge black eyes stared up from a narrow face that hadn't seen a washrag in some time. The poor child was starving. Edward couldn't help but think of his own family and his daughter, Jacqueline.

"Are you hungry?" he asked kindly. "There is plenty of food for everyone. No reason to steal."

The boy still didn't speak.

"I wonder who his family is?" Mercy knelt alongside Edward.

Guillermo glared at the boy with blatant disapproval. "He has no family. None that we have seen. He has been hanging around *Rio Concho* the past week," he added, referring to the nearby tent and shack town where the Mexican miners resided. "Eating garbage and stealing small items of value when he thought no one was around."

Mercy reached for the boy. When he flinched, she pulled back. "I won't hurt you, I promise."

He didn't move.

"If you tell me your name, I'll fix you a plate of food."

Interest flickered in his eyes. "Luiz."

"Where are your parents, Luiz?"

The boy tensed. "They are dead," he whispered.

"How terrible." Mercy stood and took his hand. This time he didn't resist. "Come. There's an empty seat over there where you can have your supper."

He started to pull away. Just as Edward renewed his grip, the boy stopped cold in his tracks. Eyes bright with wonder, he pointed to the ring hanging from a chain around Mercy's neck and uttered, "*Angel de Plata.*"

Mercy touched the ring. "What did you say?" she asked in stunned amazement. "Do you know about the Silver Angel Mine?"

He nodded reverently. "*Sí.*"

"What? Tell me."

"My family," the boy began hesitantly. Edward gave his shoulder a reassuring squeeze. "They came to Arizona looking for the *Angel de Plata.*"

"Who is your family?"

"The Rodriguezes," he said proudly.

No one reacted except Guillermo, who'd been involved in a conversation with another miner. "Ha!" He turned on Luiz. "You call yourself a Rodriguez?"

"It is true." The boy shot Guillermo a furious look. "My

name is Luiz Rodriguez. I was named after my great, great uncle. Luiz Renaldo Rodriguez."

"Who are the Rodriguezes?" Mercy asked.

Luiz refused to answer again, so Guillermo did for him. "They were a wealthy family who lived in Mexico many, many years ago. They owned much land and gold and silver mines. It is said that two of the sons and one cousin traveled to Arizona. They had heard of the *Angel de Plata* and came looking for it."

"Did they find it?" In spite of the heat and humidity, Mercy's complexion paled.

"No."

"What happened?"

"The Apache who lived in the *Mano del Diablo* Mountains believed it to be their sacred home. They ambushed the Rodriguez men and killed the brothers. The cousin escaped. At least, that is how the story goes."

"That is not true," Luiz cried out. "They did find the mine."

"Why did they not claim it then?"

"The mine is cursed," he said meekly. "My great, great uncle would not return."

"You are a liar as well as a thief." Guillermo spit in the dirt at the boy's feet. "There are many who call themselves a Rodriguez. Even though the family lost their wealth and fell to ruin, they still think the name will bring them honor. It makes me sick." He stormed off without looking back.

"I am a Rodriguez," Luiz shouted after him. "And I can prove it."

Fishing in the front pocket of his tattered pants, he pulled something out. Very slowly, he opened his hand. Nestled in the middle of his palm was a ring identical to the one Mercy wore.

* * *

"Do you think what he said about being the great nephew of Luiz Renaldo Rodriguez is true?" Mercy asked for the third time.

She stopped her chronic pacing and went to stand by Edward. Together they observed the boy. He'd been eating continuously for the past twenty minutes, pausing only long enough to swallow and breathe. Edward was genuinely concerned the boy might become violently ill.

"I do not know. From what Guillermo says, the story of the Rodriguez family is a common one."

"But the ring. How do you explain him having it in his possession?"

"Luiz is a thief. A ring is small and easily slipped into a pocket."

Edward chose his words carefully. He had an obligation to Artemis Bidwell. Their agreement stipulated that Edward protect Mercy from danger while searching for the mine, but unbeknownst to her or anyone else, there was more to their pact. He was to also hinder or discourage Mercy whenever opportunity presented itself.

Initially he'd had no problem with the agreement. The last two days, however, had changed him. The more he came to know Mercy, the more difficulty he had keeping his end of the bargain.

She was obstinate and impulsive and a walking magnet for trouble—annoying qualities, without argument. By the same token, though, she was spirited, passionate about her cause, tireless, and resourceful—all traits which earned her his respect and admiration. Her beauty aside, Edward genuinely liked Mercy. And liking her put him in the delicate position of walking a thin line between responsibilities to his family and her uncle, and his own personal wants and desires.

While he reclined against the side of a Model T Ford

belonging to the company, Mercy fidgeted, some part of her body in constant motion—feet shuffling, hands wringing, eyes darting. When she began unconsciously fiddling with the top buttons on her blouse, Edward's thinking instantly clouded. He turned the other way, resting his elbow on the hood of the truck. Unfortunately the image of her stayed with him, mingling with the memory of their kisses.

Several gulps of air restored his equilibrium. That, and concentrating on a pair of brown hawks circling in the distance, their wings spread wide to catch the air currents.

Mercy sidled up beside him. The scent of her cologne proved too great a distraction to ignore.

"I don't doubt Luiz is a thief. You caught him stealing a pie red-handed, but that was because he's starving. It doesn't necessarily mean he's lying about his great uncle giving him the ring."

Edward suspected she wanted to believe the boy, therefore, she did. "Where did the rings come from originally?"

"They were worn by the Jesuit Priests who built the *Angel de Plata* mission at the base of the mountains. Sometime in the 1750s, I think."

"Were they the ones who discovered the mine?"

"Discovered it or claimed it. Either way, they recruited the local Indians as laborers, using them to work the mine and build their mission. Some of the Indians were skilled craftsmen, and they made the rings for the priests. Whether willingly or by force, no one knows."

"The mission was eventually deserted, yes?"

"Mmm." Mercy's gaze was fixated on Luiz, who was gobbling the pie he'd tried to steal earlier.

"What happened to the priests? Did they return to Spain?"

"They died."

"Sickness?"

"No." Mercy blanched slightly. "They were massacred." She took a moment to compose herself. "After being abused by the priests for many years, the Indians revolted and killed them all. That's probably why so many people think the mine is cursed.

"How terrible." So terrible, it had taken Edward's mind off the buttons on Mercy's blouse. "How did your father acquire his ring?"

"From a rancher who lived north of here."

"How did the rancher come by it?"

"According to my father's journal, it had belonged to the rancher's wife. A family heirloom of some sort."

"And the rancher sold it?" The thought of parting with family pieces bothered Edward. The Cartiers had sold more than livestock to pay for food the last few years, but they'd managed to hold onto the few precious keepsakes they owned.

"Yes. When my father met him, the rancher was an old man. He'd married late in life and his son, his only child, was a young man. The son grew up hearing stories about the mine and was obsessed with finding it. The rancher wanted his son to settle down and take over running the ranch. That's why he sold the ring to my father. He thought if he got rid of it, his son would eventually see reason."

"Did he?"

Mercy shook her lowered head and sniffed. "They had a parting of ways. The son disappeared and, as far as anyone knew, never returned. The rancher died soon afterwards. He wound up leaving the ranch to a distant relative."

Something had obviously distressed her. "What is it, Mercy?" He touched her arm. "Are you all right?"

She looked up and smiled brightly. Too brightly. "I'm fine. It's just such a sad story."

"You lost your father. The rancher lost his son. And if

what Luiz says is true, he lost two of his family members. It sounds to me like everyone who comes in possession of a ring suffers a tragedy. Are you sure you want to keep yours?"

Her green eyes sparked, and her hand clutched the ring at her neck. "I won't ever give it up."

"And your search for the mine?"

"That too."

She caught sight of something behind him and became instantly subdued.

Glancing behind him, Edward spotted Artemis Bidwell weaving through the crowd toward them.

Mercy took Edward by the hand. "Is that invitation to dance still open?"

She'd done it again—rendered him speechless. She was quite possibly the only woman to ever accomplish that on a regular basis.

If he wasn't careful, he might develop a fondness for it.

"Of course," he said, when he recovered the power of speech, and escorted her to the dance floor.

Holding her again wasn't as enjoyable as he'd hoped. Mercy had her own reason for dancing with him, which became quickly apparent. She didn't want her uncle to hear their conversation.

"I'm going to take Luiz with us on our next trip to the *Mano del Diablo*."

Connie Bidwell had pegged her niece exactly. Regardless of her uncle's specific orders to the contrary, Mercy had every intention of returning to the mountains. Edward tried to discourage her, as was his job.

"He is just a child. What possible help can he be?"

"He can recount the stories his great uncle told him. Maybe there are clues in them. Something we've missed."

"And maybe he is a liar, as Guillermo says."

"One trip will quickly prove it or disprove it," she said

airily. "I want to leave next Saturday morning. An overnight trip this time."

"Overnight? What about your family?"

"I'll speak to them." At his curt laugh, she reiterated, "I will."

"Before or after we leave?"

She glowered at him. "I suppose you're going to tell my uncle first. You do work for him, after all."

"No."

Her brows lifted at his answer. "Is that so?"

"My job is to protect you, not interfere in your family matters."

"Uncle Artemis will have your hide if he finds out you knew I was going and didn't tell him."

"True, but since you have assured me you will speak to him, I have nothing to worry about. Yes?"

She eked out a weak, "Yes," in reply.

Clearly she didn't relish the prospect of telling her uncle, but Edward trusted her conscience would prevail. "What will you do with Luiz for the next week? Where will he stay?"

The song ended and, though Edward released her, neither of them made a move to leave the dance floor. When the music started up again, Mercy drifted back into his arms without missing a beat.

"I thought you might be willing to take care of him."

"Me!" He coughed so hard people turned to stare.

"Do you have room in your quarters? If not, I can make arrangements for a cot."

"It is not a matter of room."

"What is it then?" She gazed at him expectantly, her mouth ripe and tempting.

He looked away before he did something foolish, like kiss her. "Your uncle—if he finds out, I will lose my job."

"For taking in an orphan boy? I don't think even Uncle Artemis is that mean."

"For taking in an orphan boy and bringing him along on a trip into the mountains which he has forbidden," he reiterated. "My family is depending on me too much for me to risk losing my job."

"Fine. I understand."

"Mercy."

"Really, you don't have to take him in. I'll locate someone else." She gave a little pout. "It's just that he seems to like you, and you him."

"You are trying to . . . how do you say it? Twist my arm."

She was, but refused to admit it. "And you don't have to come with me next Saturday, either," she went on in the same wounded voice, hoping to goad him into agreeing to take Luiz. "I relieve you of your agreement with my uncle. I'll get the equipment and supplies somewhere else."

"Mercy." He stopped twirling her and they slowed to a standstill. Couples glided by in a blur of colors as they stared at one another. "Are you sure you still want me along on your prospecting trips after what happened yesterday?"

Somehow he'd managed to change the subject.

"Nearly drowning has forced me to admit I can't do this alone."

"That is not what I was asking."

"I know," she whispered. The moment of awareness between them lingered.

"And?"

"The answer is yes." She slid her left hand slightly higher on his back, bringing him that much closer. "I still want you."

Edward responded by leaning forward until their temples brushed. "I will accompany you," he said into her ear. Then he swept her into a wide turn, and they resumed dancing.

"That may be a mistake."

He knew it, but wild horses couldn't keep him away—not when she'd as much as admitted to having feelings for him.

"What about Luiz?" she asked. "Can he stay with you?"

"Will you tell your uncle about him?"

She laughed merrily. "You drive a hard bargain, Mr. Cartier."

"Why is his coming along so important to you?"

"Something tells me he's part of all this. That he has the answers I'm looking for."

"To the location of the mine?"

"Yes." Her smile faltered. "And other questions."

This time when the song ended, Edward didn't release her. "What questions?"

Inside the circle of his arms, she trembled. "Why my father died."

"He fell off a ledge."

"That's what I was told, but there are references in his journal which point to another possibility."

"What are you saying?"

She drew in an unsteady breath. "I'm saying my father may have been pushed."

Chapter Six

July 20, 1908

I visited the old mission today, as I often do on my way back into the mountains from Paradise. The condition of the building is amazing. Not one crack mars the walls. Not one timber has rotted with age. Were it not for the dust settling on the benches and tables, I'd think time had come to a complete stop in that one place on Earth.

I don't know why I go there—looking for possible clues to the mine's whereabouts, I suppose, though what I expect to find I don't know. Nothing whatsoever is left of the priests' personal belongings. The Indians must have taken everything, trading what they could, such as the rings, and destroying the rest. They were a peaceful people by nature, farmers and craftsmen who loved their families and cared nothing for wealth. I can't see them working the mine or holding onto any reminders of the people who mistreated them for decades . . .

I had to stop for a while and take a short walk. What

I wrote in the paragraph above started me thinking. I always assumed the priests hid the location of the mine in order to protect it from thieves. But what if they didn't? What if the Indians, after killing the priests, destroyed the entrance to the mine so as not to be reminded of what happened? It's something to consider.

All along I've been trying to think like a priest. Perhaps I should start thinking like an Indian.

Charles Oliver Bidwell

Mercy closed her father's journal, placed it in the drawer of the table by her bed, and blew out the candle. She'd hoped reading some of the entries would build her courage, but as she tiptoed from her room down the dark hall to the stairs, her resolve flagged with each step. She hated deceiving her aunt and uncle. If only there was another way.

A loose floorboard squeaked loudly. Mercy winced, then waited, her ears strained to hear the least little noise from her aunt and uncle's bedroom. When no one appeared, she continued down the stairs, daring to breathe only when she reached the bottom.

Something brushed against her arm, and she twisted sidewards, bumping into the railing. Heart banging like mad, she tried to focus and almost laughed out loud when she saw what had spooked her. Aunt Connie had left the parlor windows open and hung damp sheets over them in an attempt to cool the house. A breeze stirred the sheets. The one closest to her billowed out into the room, eerie as a ghost's robe.

Holding tight to the sack of provisions she'd prepared last evening and hid under her bed, Mercy padded the length of the parlor to the front door. Once outside, she'd be free to make her escape. The note she'd left on her bedside table would explain everything to her aunt and uncle—where she'd gone and why, along with an apology. She'd also absolved Edward of any blame.

Mercy had made a dozen attempts during the past week to speak to her uncle about her trip. He mostly ignored her. Only once did he acknowledge her, and then he forbid her to so much as talk about the mountains, much less return to them. She was left with no other choice but to go without his permission.

She'd told Edward of her plans to leave an hour before daybreak on Saturday. When he'd asked if she'd informed her uncle of their departure, she had told him yes, they'd had several discussions. She didn't mention that the discussions were mostly one-sided.

Frosty had arrived in Paradise unexpectedly the day before with exciting news. He'd found a sizeable nugget of black rock at a spot near the area they were looking in. He'd had the nugget examined at the assayer's office, and it was determined to be high grade silver ore. Mercy took Frosty's find as a sign they were doing the right thing.

All that stood between her and leaving was the front door of her aunt and uncle's house.

Lifting the latch quarter-inch by quarter-inch, she eased the door open and stepped outside into the marginally cooler night. It had rained three evenings in a row, and she could smell the dampness in the air.

Closing the door as carefully as she'd opened it, she allowed herself to expel a soft sigh. She'd done it. Now to meet Edward, Luiz, and Frosty at the warehouse, where the wagon and equipment were stored.

At the bottom of the porch steps, she collided with a black shape appearing from nowhere. Unable to help herself, she let out a yelp.

"Awful early to be up and about, Mercy."

"Uncle Artemis!" Her chest heaved as air rushed in and out. "You scared the life out of me."

"Serves you right, sneaking out at this ungodly hour."

"What are you doing here?"

"I'd ask you the same question, young lady, if I didn't already know the answer." He loomed over Mercy, and she felt herself involuntarily shrink. "Why don't you save us another argument and march straight back inside."

"No."

"What did you say?"

The courage Mercy had been lacking suddenly filled her. She had to make a stand, and do it now, or live the rest of her life under her uncle's thumb.

"I love you, Uncle, and I respect you, but I'm going to search for the Silver Angel Mine." She steeled herself by straightening her spine. "I hope you brought a strong rope with you, because the only way you'll stop me is to hog-tie me."

"I'm considering doing just that."

Were the shadows playing tricks on her, or had the corners of his mouth twitched? Surely he couldn't find her actions remotely amusing.

"How did you know I was leaving this morning? Did Edward tell you?"

"He's going with you then? I wondered." Uncle Artemis squinted one eye in a menacing frown. "I'd have run him off for good if he weren't."

"So he didn't tell you?"

"No."

Relief washed over her. Edward had kept his word. "Who did?"

"You."

"Me?"

"You are your father's child, Mercy. He had a lousy poker face, too. Never could hide a good hand when he had one. I figured you were up to something last night when you offered to wash the supper dishes and then took an hour to finish. It didn't require much to put two and two together."

"I tried talking to you, but you wouldn't listen."

"I'm listening now."

Her head snapped up. "You are?"

"For a man with a lot of responsibility, I can be slow sometimes. I've been up most of the night thinking about what to do."

"And?"

"I've decided you're going to search for that blasted silver mine no matter what I do or how I feel. I may be able to stop you this time and possibly the next, but you'll sneak by me sooner or later. And if I'm unlucky, you'll be mad enough to stay away for good. I can't stand it that you're chasing the same wild dreams as your father, but I don't want to lose you." He cleared his throat before continuing. "So it looks like I'll have to concede."

Mercy threw her arms around her uncle and gave him a huge bear hug. "Thank you."

He returned the hug. "I know I must seem overprotective. It comes from having three sons and no daughters."

"I promise I'll be careful," she said into the front of his shirt. "And I have lots of help. Frosty and Luiz are coming, too, along with Edward."

"Ah, yes. Cartier," he said thoughtfully and put her gently from him. "Now there's an idea that backfired on me."

"Hiring him?"

He made a grumpy sound. "He's supposed to protect you. But from what I saw at the dance last Sunday, I'm going to have to hire a second man to protect you from *him*."

It was impossible to deny the small thrill winding through her. But for the sake of her uncle, she protested. "You're being silly."

"Am I? I don't think so. Neither does your Aunt Connie. She's concerned you might be in over your head."

"Tell her not to fret."

"Does that mean you're not interested in Cartier?"

"Of course I'm not interested in him," she said, pleased at how glibly she lied.

He clamped a hand to the back of his head and groaned. "There goes that lousy poker face of yours again."

So much for being a glib liar. When he stalked off, she ran after him. "Where are you going?"

"The warehouse. Isn't that where you're meeting your cohorts in crime?"

She had to jog to keep pace with him. "You're not going to embarrass me by lecturing Edward, are you?"

"Young lady, I do not lecture."

"And chickens don't lay eggs."

"Didn't they teach you better manners in that fancy girls' school?"

"Please, Uncle Artemis."

"I'm not going to lecture him," he groused, then drew up so quickly Mercy barely avoided knocking into him. Scowling at her, he said, "But if he makes even the slightest improper suggestion to you, I'll do a whole lot more than lecture him. He'll feel the sole of my boot in his hind end all the way from here to Canada. You hear me?"

"Is that why you brought your gun?" she asked with a touch of defiance. "To intimidate Edward?" She'd felt the outline of the revolver he sometimes wore at his side when they'd hugged.

"No, that's not why I brought my gun." His scowl dissolved into a look of tenderness. "Mostly you remind me of your father, but I see a little of your mother in you, too. She also had a bit of a sharp tongue."

They began walking again, this time at a more reasonable

speed. In the distance, the outline of the power house chimneys stretched high like two arms reaching for the stars. Wisps of steam floated from the mouths of the chimneys, only to dissolve into nothingness. During the day, it would pour out in a thick, continuous stream, clogging the air surrounding the mining complex with acrid fumes.

"Tell me about my mother," Mercy said.

"She was a beautiful woman. Kind and compassionate." He chuckled. "Your father was smitten with her from the first moment he laid eyes on her at the Hollybrook County Fair. That never changed. He loved her as much the day he died as the day they were wed."

"I know. He writes about her in his journal."

Uncle Artemis's face softened. "A part of him died, too, when he lost her. I can't say I liked him searching for that mine, but it did give him a reason to crawl out of bed every morning. And while I would have never wished your mother ill, I did enjoy having my younger brother around. When he was here, that is—he spent most of his time in those mountains."

"At least you saw him occasionally."

"I'd forgotten you hadn't seen him since you were . . . what?" Uncle Artemis looked forlorn. "Twelve?"

"Thereabouts." Mercy knew exactly how old she was the last time she'd seen her father, but she didn't tell her uncle that. Pain squeezed her heart as she asked the question which had been tearing at her for years. "Why did he leave me in Boston? Why didn't he bring me here to live with you and Aunt Connie?"

"We'd have taken you in, for sure, but he didn't think Arizona was a suitable place to raise a young girl. Your mother was an educated woman, and he wanted as much for you."

Or maybe he just plain didn't want me.

Uncle Artemis must have sensed her despair, for he placed an arm around her shoulder. "You know, finding that mine—if it does exist—won't bring him back."

"But it will prove he wasn't a crackpot like people say."

"Is that why you're so intent on finding it?"

"One of the reasons."

"What are the others?"

Mercy considered telling her uncle about her suspicions and decided against it. If Uncle Artemis thought for one second her father was murdered, he'd refuse to let her return to the mountains and they'd be back to where they started. So she gave him a different answer.

"Money."

"Money! You think the mine will make you rich?"

She huffed at his comical double take. "Stranger things have happened."

"And what would you do with all that wealth?"

Ignoring his sarcastic tone, she said, "Travel, for one thing. First I'd see everything there is to see here, then I'd go abroad. After the war, of course. It's not safe right now." She let her imagination wander. "Rome, I think, and Paris. Maybe even Switzerland. After all this desert, I'll be ready for lots and lots of snow."

"Those are some mighty fine aspirations."

"Yes," she said dreamily, still envisioning snow-capped mountains.

"Assuming you do find this mythical mine, where will you get the capital to reopen it?"

"Capital . . . ?"

"I hate to be the bearer of bad news, but that silver ore won't jump out of the ground into your hands all by itself."

"Well, I . . ." Mercy had no response. The truth was, she hadn't thought that far ahead.

"You're going to need capital to fund your operation until

you make a strike. There are geologists and engineers to hire, and equipment to buy. You'll need laborers when the time comes to start digging. And armed guards to keep out any riffraff. How will you pay for all that?"

"I don't know," she said, trying to absorb everything. A few weeks ago the cost of prospecting equipment and supplies had daunted her. Compared to the cost of reopening a mine, that was peanuts. Well, at least Uncle Artemis was talking like she might actually locate the mine. There was something to be said for that. "Could I sell shares?"

"Possibly. I'm not so sure the old man wouldn't be interested," he said, referring to Thatcher Newlin, the owner of the Paradise Consolidated Copper Company. "You could always approach him. The worst he can say is no."

They rounded a corner, and the warehouse came into sight. Standing in front were three figures, one of them significantly shorter than the other two; Edward, Frosty, and Luiz.

The tallest figure stepped forward, triggering the familiar fluttering in Mercy's chest. Edward. Was he really as smitten with her as her uncle indicated?

She tried to read his face. What did he think about seeing Uncle Artemis? He didn't appear surprised, or perhaps he hid it well. She gave him credit for not turning on his heels and running away—but then, she didn't really expect him to. Edward hardly impressed her as the type of man who feared a confrontation.

"Good morning, gentlemen," Uncle Artemis said when they were within speaking range.

"Morning." Edward tipped his hat.

Frosty removed his. Luiz hid behind Edward, peering out with big brown eyes lit with trepidation. It hadn't taken the boy long to learn who was in charge around Paradise.

Mercy commended herself for insisting Edward house the

boy. He'd blossomed during the past week. A bath and a new set of clothes had produced a minor miracle, vastly improving his appearance—that, and three square meals a day. He obviously adored Edward, and Mercy guessed the feeling was reciprocated to a certain degree.

With a little coaxing, which included three peppermint sticks, Mercy had persuaded Luiz to open up one afternoon at the office and tell her some stories about his family in his halting English. From Luiz's descriptions, she was convinced his great uncle had visited the *Mano del Diablo* Mountains. Whether he'd actually found the mine as Luiz insisted remained to be seen.

Someone had already fetched Samson and tied him to a post. At Mercy's approach, the mule raised his head and snorted a greeting. She responded by scratching him behind his long ears.

Uncle Artemis braced his hands on his hips and assessed the men. "Embarking on a little trip, I see."

"Yes, sir."

Edward didn't appear one bit perturbed, and Mercy once again had the impression something was going on with the two men.

"Uncle Artemis has come to see us off."

"Not exactly, Mercy."

She didn't like the innuendo in her uncle's voice. He was up to something. "You're not?"

"No." His grin stretched from ear to ear. "I'm going with you."

Mercy's jaw fell open. "You're joking."

"Not in the least. You don't mind, do you?"

She minded very much. "N—no. Of course n—not."

"What about you, Cartier?"

The two men eyed each other. "Happy to have you along," Edward replied.

"Good. It's settled then. Shall we get started?"

Edward and Uncle Artemis each took hold of a handle on the large double door to the warehouse and pulled. It rolled open with a loud screech.

"Someone have a light?" Uncle Artemis asked, stepping inside the darkened building.

Edward struck a match and lit a lantern which sat atop a small shelf beside the door. He adjusted the knob until the flame caught and grew. In the next instant, the room was bathed in yellow light.

"What in tarnation happened here?" Uncle Artemis roared.

Mercy sucked in a startled breath and stared at the wagon in disbelief, her stomach turning to lead. The entire contents had been ransacked and tossed onto the floor, some of the items broken and in pieces.

Frosty let out a low whistle. "Looks like you've been robbed."

"I do not think so." Edward stepped into the middle of the mess and picked up a sack which had been turned inside out. He then nudged a toppled water jug with his foot. "Everything has been gone through, but nothing is missing from what I can see."

"Why would someone do this?" Mercy cried, stooping down to right an overturned crate.

Edward dropped the sack after inspecting it. "They were searching for something. Something they did not find." He looked at her, his brows lifted in question. "Do you know what it might be?"

She could do little more than blink, so great was her astonishment. "I don't have the faintest idea."

Chapter Seven

January 8, 1915

I'm on first watch tonight, and Frosty is on second. When we returned from digging this afternoon it was to find our camp had been ransacked. Naturally, we assumed we'd fallen victim to a gang of thieves. We were wrong.

As it so happens, nothing was missing—which rules out bandits or renegade Indians, both of whom use the twisting canyons in these mountains as hideouts. Bootleggers ignore us as long as we ignore them, and claim-jumpers are more apt to attack at digging sites. Who did this remains a mystery.

I admit I'm starting to worry. Last month, we twice noticed a rider following us in the distance and not many days later, shots were fired over our heads. Someone is trying to scare us off.

Frosty and I talked at supper tonight and are in com-

plete agreement. We are committed to finding the mine despite the risks. We must be close, or else why would this person be taking such drastic measures?

It sounds preposterous, but I can't help thinking the rancher's son, young Mr. Houseman, is involved. He is an obsessed man, and obsessed men will go to any lengths to get what they want.

Just look at me.

Charles Oliver Bidwell

By the time the rising sun crested the horizon, they'd cleaned up the mess in the warehouse and reloaded the wagon. Mercy assumed Uncle Artemis would cancel their trip. To her surprise, he didn't, and insisted they leave as scheduled. As he put it, "I'm not about to let some two-bit troublemaker scare us off."

Because five people were more of a load than old Samson could pull, it was agreed that Frosty, Mercy, and Luiz would take the wagon while Edward and Uncle Artemis rode horses. Mercy couldn't decide if she liked the arrangement or not. Half of her was relieved at not having to battle the disquieting emotions Edward's proximity always evoked in her. The other half missed those same disquieting emotions.

What was wrong with her? From the start, Edward affected her like no other man. Her heart, she feared, was choosing unwisely. They were unsuited for each other for many reasons, not the least of which being he would someday return to Canada to be with his family. And what about her? If they found the mine, she could conceivably become a rich woman and be able to travel as she wanted.

For the first time since her arrival in Paradise last March, the notion of leaving filled Mercy with sadness rather than joy. Something must *really* be wrong with her, and she suspected that something rode just ahead astride a stout bay mare.

At the river, Samson balked as usual. Before Frosty could climb down to fetch Buttercup to lead the stubborn mule across the river, Edward stopped him.

"Wait, *mon ami*. I have an idea."

"What's that?"

"Luiz." Edward beckoned the boy. "Come here."

Exuberance lighting his face, Luiz scrambled down from the wagon. Edward dismounted and handed his reins over to Uncle Artemis.

"Can you ride a horse?" Edward asked, and Luiz nodded enthusiastically. "What about a mule?"

The boy studied Samson critically. "He does not look much different."

"Not much different at all." Edward ruffled Luiz's hair, then picked him up and deposited him on Samson's back. "Hold onto this." He placed the boy's hands on the leather collar. "When I tell you, I want you to kick him in the sides. Hard," he emphasized. "Can you do that?"

Another nod.

"Good." He patted Luiz on the leg before mounting his horse. After a brief word to Uncle Artemis, the two men rode up to the wagon and positioned their horses, one on either side of Samson. When they were all set, Edward motioned for them to move ahead and spurred his horse.

Frosty clucked to the mule and snapped the reins while Luiz kicked and shouted encouragements. Edward and Uncle Artemis urged their horses into the river. Samson raised his head high, his ears flicking back and forth. Then, with a loud snort, he followed, plowing into the river at full speed. The wagon rattled and pitched as it went over the rocky bottom. Water splashed, drenching Mercy and Frosty, but they didn't care and merely laughed with wild abandon. At the top of the bank on the other side, they stopped to rest.

"Well, I'll be," Frosty said. "Weren't that something?"

Edward rode up beside the heavily breathing mule and reached a hand to Luiz. "Well done." He lifted the boy from Samson's back.

His small face split in half by a huge grin, Luiz climbed onto the horse behind Edward. "That was fun. Can we do it again?"

"Of course we can. On the way back."

Edward looked around, making sure everyone was account-ed for, then nudged his horse into a trot. Luiz hung on, his short legs dangling, and his skinny arms locked around Edward.

Mercy was profoundly moved by the sight of them together. She'd been very wrong in her assumption that Edward wasn't a family man. His daughter was a lucky little girl. And though it would mean she'd never see him again, Mercy hoped Jacqueline and her father were soon reunited.

A man who treats children with such kindness would make a wonderful husband. Mercy ignored the voice inside her head. She didn't want to think about Edward and his late wife. Late wife? Who was she fooling? She'd been thinking about herself as Edward's wife, and warming to the idea much too much for her own good.

As a means of distraction, she concentrated on Frosty. The old prospector was telling tales about a notorious band of outlaws—rebel deserters—who supposedly inhabited the region north of them half a century ago, wreaking mayhem on the locals until the authorities drove them out.

When they neared the place where Frosty found his silver nugget, Luiz started bouncing up and down, almost falling off the horse in his excitement. Pointing to the top of a rocky ledge, he shouted, "Look. There are the angel wings."

"What angel wings?" she asked.

"At the very top. See how the rocks come together to make wings?"

This was new information to Mercy. She didn't remember running across anything like it in her father's journal. Scanning the mountainside, she tried desperately to catch a glimpse of whatever had Luiz in such a state.

Squirming to free both arms, he formed his hands into the shape of wings. "My great uncle told me about the wings. He said that is how the mine got its name."

Then she saw them, and a chill danced up her spine. With a certainty she couldn't explain, she knew they were near the mine. It was as if her father spoke to her from heaven above.

She'd been right to bring Luiz along on their trip. He would be a big help. "Stop the wagon," she cried, and Frosty did. "We'll make camp here."

No one talked much, each setting about their individual tasks. After unharnessing Samson, they tied him and the horses among a stand of mesquite trees. Next, they loaded Buttercup's pack saddle with the supplies and equipment they'd need for the day. By then, they were all good and hungry.

They took their lunch in camp. Edward removed the seat from the wagon and set it on the ground for Mercy and Uncle Artemis. The rest of them found a spot wherever they could. Luiz finished ahead of the others and went wandering, with strict instructions to remain nearby. Mercy envied him. Something about this place called her—the distant screech of a hawk, the buzzing of insects, the rustling of shrubs—all carried the same invitation to come and explore.

While the men debated the best direction to begin searching, she hiked to the backside of the ledge.

Was it her imagination, or did a footpath lead to the rock wings? Yes, there was a footpath! Incredible!

Following the steeply winding path, she climbed the rise, skirting prickly cacti and avoiding those places which dropped off sharply. The footpath soon brought her to a small, flat mesa directly above the rock wings. There, the trail ended. Even with her lack of experience, Mercy could see she'd reached a dead end.

Disappointment filled her. Well, what had she expected? That she'd come up here and find the opening to the mine just waiting for her? Of course not. And yet . . .

She walked to the edge of the mesa. The rock wings were directly below her. Were she brave enough, she could reach out and touch the tips. Mercy wasn't that brave and instead found a boulder to sit on, one that afforded her a spectacular view. Her thoughts soon began to drift.

Had Indians used this place for religious ceremonies because it was close to their god and nature? Or maybe outlaws and warring Apaches hid behind the very boulder she sat on, waiting to ambush their enemies. Small details of their camp were clearly visible, she noted, and voices carried a long distance.

A flash of color drew her attention, and she craned her neck to see. On the ridge just below, a red fox darted through the shrub carrying a limp jackrabbit in its mouth. Mercy decided the fox must be taking food to her cubs. It made straight for the center of the rock wings, then disappeared, presumably into her den.

"Look at that," she muttered to herself.

"Look at what?"

Mercy jerked upright and plopped back down at the sight of Edward. "You gave me a start."

He sat on a boulder next to hers. In his lap he placed a small bundle secured by a red handkerchief. "You have been gone a long time. We were beginning to worry."

"I'm fine. Just exploring some."

"You did not eat much at lunch."

Leave it to Edward to notice when no one else did. "I'm too excited to eat," she said.

"You will need your strength this afternoon if you expect to go prospecting with us. We have a lot of ground to cover before we must head home." He untied the handkerchief and removed a tin can with no label and two spoons.

"What's this?" she asked when he handed her a spoon.

He shrugged. "A whole shipment of cans came into the company store with no labels. The manager did not know what was in the cans, so he sold them for half-price. Luiz eats a lot," Edward said with a smile, "and he is not picky. I think sometimes he will starve me out of house and home."

Mercy suffered a pang of guilt. "I'm sorry."

"For what?" He removed a can opener from his pants pocket.

"It was inconsiderate of me to insist you take him in. The cost of feeding a growing boy didn't occur to me. I know how hard you're working at saving money for your family. I'll find a way to repay you."

"That is not necessary. He earns his keep. I have not washed one dish or swept the house since he came to stay." Edward popped the lid from the can and examined the contents, his expression wary. "How brave are you?"

Mercy remembered her earlier caution when approaching the rock wings. "Not very." Cold beans or spinach didn't appeal to her.

He took a spoonful and grimaced as he swallowed. "For half-price, I suppose I can get used to it." He offered her the can. "Here. Try some."

She recoiled. "No, thank you."

"Go on." He pushed the can at her. "You need to eat."

"Really, Edward. I'm not hungry." She peeked at the open

can through slitted eyes, then punched him lightly on the arm, which made him laugh. "It's applesauce." No longer needing to be coaxed, she tried a small taste. The applesauce was both sweet and tart and melted on her tongue.

He had another spoonful, and his contented smile told her that he agreed. They took turns dipping into the can. At one point their spoons clicked and tangled. From the ribbon of sensation shooting up Mercy's arm, it might have been their fingers touching.

"Excuse me." She removed her spoon as a familiar heat flooded her cheeks.

Edward lifted his spoon from the can, but instead of eating the applesauce, he offered it to Mercy.

She hesitated. The act of sharing food like this was—in some ways—as intimate as kissing. His eyes burned with what she recognized as desire. In response, her pulse soared, the beat of it echoing in her temples. She opened her mouth, and Edward's spoon slipped inside. The same spoon which, moments before, had been in his mouth.

Applesauce never tasted so good.

The warm metal slid over her teeth as he removed the spoon. With trembling hands, she dipped her own spoon into the applesauce. Just as she raised it to his lips, a high-pitched scream rent the air.

In the next instant they were on their feet and racing down the narrow footpath to camp.

"Do not move," Edward said with calm assurance, "and do not talk."

Luiz pressed his back into a boulder, his face white as chalk. In the sand directly at his feet lay a giant diamondback, its tail rattling in a distinct sign of agitation. Slowly, and with deadly grace, the snake slithered in and out of a tight coil, poised and ready to strike.

Edward's alarm at hearing Luiz cry out paled next to the terror seizing him now.

Behind him, Artemis Bidwell removed his revolver from his holster and cocked it. Frosty stood on the other side of Edward, and behind him, Mercy. He could hear her rapid, shallow breathing and prayed that just this once she'd obey orders and stay back.

"How good is your aim?" Edward asked Artemis Bidwell.

"Good enough, if that forked-tongue son of Satan will just hold still."

That wasn't quite the answer Edward wanted to hear, but they didn't have much choice. He considered using the knife he carried in his right boot, then decided that even without perfect aim, they had a better chance with the gun.

Luiz made a panicked sound and tried to crawl backwards up the bolder, digging the heels of his shoes into the rock.

"Stay still," Edward all but shouted, then lowered his voice. "It is very important, son, that you do not move."

The rattling increased in volume. Edward's blood ran cold when he realized the reason. Another snake, possibly more than one, lay in the cracks beneath the boulder, mere inches from Luiz's leg.

Waiting out the danger ceased being an option.

"Do you see his friend there?" Edward said over his shoulder to Artemis Bidwell. He tried to act nonchalant, not wanting to upset Luiz any more than he already was. The boy was literally shaking all over, and Edward feared his constant movements would provoke the snakes into attacking. "He must have disturbed their rest while playing on the rocks."

"I see him," the mine superintendent replied.

"What should we do?"

"Get him out of there. The way he keeps kicking up sand and stones, it's only a matter of time."

Edward agreed.

The image of a snake sinking its fangs into Luiz's leg turned Edward's blood to ice. Given his small size, Luiz might not survive. Edward vowed not to let that happen. Somehow, someway, they'd save the boy. The biggest obstacle facing them was fear; their fear of the snakes, and the snakes' fear of them.

"Are you ready?" Edward asked.

"Let's do it," Artemis Bidwell answered.

"Look at me, Luiz, and listen carefully." Edward waited until the boy raised his head. His brown eyes were wide and fathomless. "We will get you out of here, but you must do everything exactly as I tell you to. Do you understand?"

He nodded, his frightened gaze wavering back and forth from Edward to the snake at his feet.

"On the count of three, I am going to jump in and grab you. When I do, you throw your arms around my neck and hold on as tight as you can." Edward spoke to Luiz, but his words were for the benefit of everyone there. He could hear them in the background, quietly shifting into position. "Mr. Bidwell is going to shoot the snake in the head."

Luiz whimpered.

"Do not be scared," Edward reassured him. "You and I will be safe. I move much faster than that old snake." He hoped it was true.

"Be careful," Luiz whispered.

"I will." Edward glanced sideways at Artemis Bidwell and saw him nod. "Here we go, then. On the count of three. One . . . two . . ." He inched forward. "Three!"

Before the word left his mouth, he dove at Luiz. The boy did as he was told and lifted his arms, wrapping them around Edward's neck. Artemis Bidwell fired the gun at the same instant Edward felt a piercing stab in his left calf. Swinging Luiz off the ground, he spun in a circle and ran for all he was worth. Pain exploded up the length of his calf, but he didn't stop.

"Frosty!" he called.

The old prospector appeared beside him and took Luiz. Edward managed three more steps before his leg gave out and he collapsed on his knees. He refused to disgrace himself by falling face first in the sand.

Mon Dieu. The sun was hot. What happened to his hat? He'd been wearing it a minute ago.

"Cartier! Are you all right?" Artemis Bidwell shouted to him from what sounded like a great distance away.

How strange.

Mercy's face floated in front of him. Even with her brow creased in a deep frown, she was pretty. So very pretty. He wanted to kiss her, and promised himself he would the next time they were alone.

"Edward." She laid a cool hand on his cheek.

He felt like he was on fire, and his leg throbbed. "How is Luiz?" He thought of asking about the snakes, but at that point, they didn't matter.

"Luiz is fine, thanks to you." She grabbed Edward's shirt front as he started to sway. "Tell me what to do." Her voice rose an octave. "I don't know how to treat a rattlesnake bite."

"I am not bit." He tried to chuckle, but only succeeded in making a harsh, croaking noise. "Your uncle shot me."

Edward settled the straight-back chair between his knees. If he were ever going to escape this blasted infirmary, he'd have to be able to walk, at least a short distance. To walk, he had to first stand. Gripping the top of the chair back, he hauled himself to his feet.

It was sheer agony. Worse than the ride back to Paradise yesterday in the bed of that old wagon.

Hopping on his good leg, he waited for his blurred vision

to clear. Then he buttoned up the front of his pants, which had taken him a good five minutes to put on.

One day in this miserable place was enough. He'd had it with the lousy food, the lumpy bed, and the so-called gown they'd tried forcing him to wear. Never mind the sadistic doctor who took great pleasure in sticking Edward with small, sharp objects.

Luiz and Frosty were returning shortly, and Edward would insist on being released in their care. The boy had hardly left his side all night. When Thomas and Guillermo visited last evening after supper, Luiz slunk off to the corner and sat huddled in the chair. Even groggy, Edward couldn't help noticing the glaring animosity between the boy and Guillermo. He didn't understand why two relative strangers should dislike each other so intensely. If Luiz continued to stay with him, he'd have to get to the bottom of it.

But for now, he needed to focus all his attention on walking. Inhaling deeply, he pushed off and made it as far as the foot of the bed before his leg buckled. The idea of sitting was tempting, however, he resisted. Bracing his hand on the bed's metal footboard, he rested and listened for any sign of the nurse. As the infirmary's sole occupant, he was too often the object of her undivided attention.

The doctor had given Edward strict orders to rest. The bullet, he'd been told, had passed through the fleshy part of his calf. Had it struck bone, he wouldn't be standing today, if ever again. Fortunately for him, Artemis Bidwell was indeed a lousy shot.

The mine superintendent had gone out of his way to insure Edward's comfort and see that he received the best care the Paradise Consolidated Copper Company Hospital could offer.

Edward appreciated it. He especially appreciated the full pay Mr. Bidwell promised for as long as he was laid up. The possibility of lost income concerned Edward. From the letter his brother recently sent him, the Cartier family was making strides toward financial recovery. Any setback, even a small one, could mean having to start all over again.

Edward would do everything in his power to prevent that from happening. Two years away from Jacqueline had been more than enough. If all went well, they'd be together again in time for Christmas.

Using the footboard for support, he limped up the other side of the bed. Though he put as little weight on his leg as possible, the pain was crippling. At this rate, he'd never leave the infirmary. He wondered which was worse, a rattlesnake bite or a gunshot wound.

"Just what do you think you're doing?" rang a female voice.

Edward sighed, resigned to his fate. He'd been so worried about the nurse, he hadn't considered a visit from Mercy.

She charged toward him, the heels of her shoes clicking on the wooden floors. Her hat, the one she'd worn at the dance with all the flowers and feathers, flopped up and down on her head.

Edward guessed she'd come to the infirmary directly from church. And by the look on her face, she'd brought some of the preacher's fire and brimstone with her.

She stopped short and stared at his bare chest for several seconds, then promptly collected herself. "Why in heaven's name are you out of bed? Have you lost your mind? Does the doctor know?" She put an arm around his waist and wedged her shoulder under his arm, offering her body for support.

Edward acted like the short walk around the bed had taken a terrible toll on him and leaned heavily on her. She felt good. She smelled even better. Giving into impulse, he lowered his head to her neck and inhaled.

"Nice."

"Edward." She drew his name out over several syllables, her warning implicit. "What if someone sees us?"

"I will claim to be sleepwalking."

"I'm serious."

"There is only one nurse on duty. She thinks I am resting."

"You fooled her? How could you?"

"She is as stiff as her starched white uniform. I do not like her."

Encouraged that Mercy didn't knock him on his rump, Edward nuzzled her cheek. The pain in his leg became a distant memory. He suddenly remembered his promise to himself to kiss her at the first opportunity. Edward wasn't one to break a promise.

Cupping her cheek, he tilted her head and brought her mouth within inches of his.

"We shouldn't do this," she whispered, but made no move to push him away.

"Give me one good reason." His fingers curled around the column of her neck

Her eyelids fluttered, then drifted closed. "I can't think of a single one right now."

"In that case . . ." He swept his lips over hers in a light caress. Far from sated, he angled his head and kissed her more fully, liking that she stood on her tiptoes and willingly matched his ardor.

Nothing the doctor had done, no medicines they'd given him, made him feel half as good as kissing Mercy. What would it be like to begin and end each day of his life kissing her? Not a hardship by any stretch of the imagination. What *would* be hard—harder than he thought possible—was leaving her when the time came to return home.

His sense of right and wrong kicked in, and he broke off the kiss.

She traced his jaw line with her fingertips. "How about we get you back into bed?"

"Are you sure about that?" His suggestive tone gave her innocent remark a completely different meaning.

"Oh, Edward." She admonished him with a hopeless sigh and maneuvered him toward the center of the bed. "You're impossible."

He inadvertently stepped down too hard. The searing pain to his injured leg caused him to double over.

"Watch it!" Mercy caught him. "Are you all right?"

"Yes." He was now. Her closeness did more for him than all of the doctor's treatments put together.

"I can't believe Uncle Artemis shot you in the leg. What if he killed you?"

"There was little chance of that," Edward said with humor. "The wound is far from my heart." Mercy helped him turn around so he could sit down.

"You shouldn't make light of something so serious," she said with a smile.

He didn't smile back. "I do not *make light* of serious matters."

His remark stopped her. Their gazes connected, and stayed connected, as Edward lowered himself onto the bed, taking her with him. A lead ball the size of his fist lodged in his chest. It bothered him that he couldn't be honest with Mercy regarding his business arrangement with her uncle, but he was bound by agreement to remain silent.

His feelings for her, though, were an entirely different matter, and nothing prevented him revealing what lay in his heart.

Taking her hand, he kissed the palm, then pressed it to the side of his face. "If things were different," he started, "if I were not returning to Canada soon, I would . . ." His throat closed as he considered what he was about to confess.

"You would what?" she prompted.

"I . . . I . . . would call on you, Mercy."

In the four years since Anne-Marie's death, he had never considered marrying again. That he did so now, with Mercy, amazed him. Their chances of having a future together were nigh onto impossible.

"Oh, Edward." Her eyes glimmered, but her smile was sad.

"I will not make a promise I cannot keep," he said apologetically.

"I wouldn't expect you to."

"But I would give my right arm to be able to make that promise."

As if pulled by an invisible string, they moved toward each other. Wrong as it might be, he was going to kiss her one last time. Mercy sealed their fates when she tipped her face up and parted her lips. He required no further incentive and covered her mouth with his. When she eased her arms around his bare waist, he pressed her back into the headboard, taking the kiss further than the previous one.

And she let him.

It was incredible. With Mercy, Edward discovered a passion unlike any he'd known with his late wife. It scared him as much as it excited him. Could he really leave Mercy after this? How could he not?

They sprang apart when Artemis Bidwell's booming voice filled the room.

"What in blue thunder is going on here?" The mine superintendent stormed toward them, his wife and the nurse a few paces behind. "Cartier, I demand an explanation. And it had better be good."

"Uncle Artemis!" Mercy jumped off the bed, desperately rearranging her crooked hat and mussed hair.

Edward ignored his injured leg and stood. This was his fault, and he refused to let Mercy take any of the blame. His reputation could withstand a scandal, but not hers. She would be ruined in a matter of days.

"Rest assured, Mr. Bidwell, my intentions concerning your niece are very honorable."

"Is that so?" Fists clenched at his sides, Artemis Bidwell visibly restrained his anger. "They didn't look honorable from where I was standing."

Edward straightened his shoulders to the best of his ability and looked his boss square in the face. "May I have your permission to court your niece?"

From beside him, Mercy gasped.

Chapter Eight

August 3, 1911

If Esther had lived, today would be our twentieth wedding anniversary. I suppose it's natural that thoughts of her should fill my head and heart.

There are times when I almost convince myself I am a contented man. Just this evening a harvest moon rose in the eastern sky, huge and bright and so close I swear I could have touched the smiling face of the mythical man residing there. Only a hardened skeptic would not be inspired by such a sight and, for a brief moment, my spirits were lifted.

It didn't last. The truth of the matter is I miss my wife with every breath I take and will until the day I die. Fourteen years with her wasn't enough. Still, I'd gladly take fourteen years with her than three lifetimes with any other woman.

If there is one wish I have for my daughter, Mercy, it's that she finds a man who will love her as much as I

107

loved her mother. I don't know if something like that is possible, but I pray for it nightly. She deserves a good husband and a good life after having lost both parents, one to fever and one to despair.

Charles Oliver Bidwell

"Why, this is just so exciting! And such a surprise!" From her place at the dining table in the Bidwell's kitchen, Sara Jane Ketchem sent a sparkling smile first to Mercy and then to Edward. The young woman had accompanied her parents to the Bidwells for Sunday dinner. "I declare, the two of you should be scolded for keeping your romance a secret. Who would have thought it? I never did. Neither did anyone in Paradise, I can tell you that. Why didn't you say something, Mercy?" Sara Jane complained with feigned annoyance. "I'll never understand you Easterners. Always so prim and proper."

Mercy wished with all her might for the floor to open up and swallow their dinner guest whole. With everyone's eyes at the table on her—Edward's included—she was forced to pick through Sara Jane's myriad comments and respond to one.

"Well . . . it was something of a surprise to me, too."*To say the least*! She'd been flabbergasted.

"It's sweet. Isn't it sweet?" Sara Jane's gaze lighted on one person, then another, seeking confirmation. She beamed at the nods of agreement she received. "You'll simply have to come over to the house soon so I can show you my mail order catalogues. There's sections with all sorts of beautiful wedding dresses. Oops!" She covered her mouth in an exaggerated display of mortification. "Maybe Edward hasn't popped the question yet. I hope I didn't spoil anything."

Mercy doubted it. Sara Jane probably took enormous pleasure in spoiling as many things as she could. She really had no idea when to shut up. But what else could one expect from the town's most notorious gossip? Mercy tolerated the feather-brained Sara Jane out of respect for her aunt and uncle, though that tolerance was being sorely tested. Beneath the table, her linen napkin bore the brunt of her frustration and humiliation. At Sara Jane's last remark, Mercy almost ripped the helpless square of cloth in two.

News of the mine superintendent's niece and the Canadian foreman's courtship followed so closely on the heels of the mine superintendent shooting the same foreman in the leg, that the local gossips were in a frenzy. Sara Jane was the principal instigator. It was Aunt Connie's idea to have Edward join them for Sunday dinner with the Ketchems. Mercy had attempted to dissuade her aunt, who'd argued, "Seeing as you and Edward are sweet on each other, it's reasonable for him to call on you and your family."

How had they gotten into this mess? And more importantly, how were they going to get out?

Surely he planned on ending their pretend courtship soon. His announcement in the infirmary had been a spur of the moment remedy to spare her potential embarrassment . . . or so she thought. And now, thanks to the likes of Sara Jane and the ward nurse, the incident had been blown out of proportion. Somehow, some way, she and Edward must rectify matters—and promptly.

If not, what then? Would they continue their pretense to save face? A small—no, make that a large—part of her was thrilled by the notion, as wrong as she knew it to be. She contemplated him from behind lowered lashes. He didn't act like a man *pretending* to be paying her court. In fact, he'd been most convincing in his attentions to her this afternoon. She pressed her hand to her middle and resolved to speak with him soon. Today, if possible.

The Bidwells had a full house. In addition to Sara Jane,

her two younger brothers, and their parents, Mort Carmichael had also been invited. He and Sara Jane were to be married in six weeks, and Aunt Connie had agreed to help organize the wedding.

Fortunately, the dinner topic turned to Sara Jane's and Mort's impending nuptials. Mercy was able to enjoy her first moment of peace since the meal started—until Edward looked at her, his mouth curled in a sensuous half-grin.

Her poor napkin endured yet another thrashing.

"May I take your plate?" she asked him thirty minutes later when they'd finished with dessert, grateful the hand she extended didn't shake.

"Nonsense." Aunt Connie reached around Mercy and snatched Edward's plate. "You fixed practically the entire dinner. Laura, Sara Jane, and I will clean up. Why don't you two visit on the front porch?" She winked at Mercy. "Surely you must be wanting some time alone."

"By all means." Sara Jane giggled loudly. "Mother and I will help Mrs. Bidwell."

Mercy snuck a peek at Edward. Here was the opportunity she'd been waiting for. He seemed inclined to go along with Aunt Connie's none too subtle prompting. Perhaps he had another, more personal, reason. She tried to quiet the unrealistic hope building inside her.

He limped as they made their way through the parlor, and she commented on it. "Your leg is healing nicely. When Aunt Connie and I came by to visit you on Thursday, you could hardly walk."

The only time Mercy had seen Edward all week, Aunt Connie had accompanied her. Simple small talk had been awkward enough in front of her aunt, she hadn't dared broached the sensitive subject of their courtship.

"I have a confession to make, Mercy."

Her heart skipped. "What's that?"

"I was able to walk well enough."

"Then why didn't you?"

His expression resembled that of a naughty little boy caught with his finger in the cake icing. "Would you have brought me two peach pies if I weren't bedridden?"

"Oh, Edward!" She laughed, and the strain from dinner magically evaporated. "Since you're recovered, I don't suppose you require my assistance in sitting."

"I believe I have had a sudden relapse." He hopped on his good leg and grimaced unconvincingly.

Pushing him down into one of the two wicker rockers outside the front door, she said, "Then you'd best stay off your feet."

He reached over and pulled the other rocker closer to his. "Only if you join me."

She did.

Long shadows stretched across the yard, heralding the approaching evening. For some minutes, they listened to the drone of buzzing cicadas and watched the neighbor tend his flock of chickens. The earlier need to talk had ceased being important.

Eventually, Mercy broke the companionable silence with a safe subject. "If you don't mind me asking, is something amiss with you and Mort Carmichael? I couldn't help but notice he's put out with you."

"Work problems."

His ambiguous answer piqued Mercy's interest. She didn't particularly care for the engineer. His cocksure attitude irritated her. "He's on your crew, isn't he? I hear he's very good at his job."

"Yes, he is good."

Another ambiguous answer. Something was definitely amiss. "Did you have a disagreement?"

"Yes."

"About what?"

He stared at her, his mouth tight-lipped. "Work."

Obviously, he didn't care to discuss the problem with her, and she couldn't fault him. It really was none of her business. "When are you returning to work?

"Tomorrow."

"You can't be serious. For Pete's sake, Edward, you're still limping."

"My leg is stronger every day."

"Why the rush? Uncle Artemis agreed to pay you during your convalescence."

Three deep creases furrowed his forehead. "I do not take charity."

"That's just plain stubborn of you. You'll wind up hurting yourself all over again if you're not careful."

When he didn't answer, she crossed her arms and pushed hard with the ball of her feet. Her see-sawing rocking chair creaked loudly from the effects. She saw him watching her from the corner of his eye and quipped, "What are you looking at?"

"I am waiting."

"For what?"

"For you to ask me about what happened in the infirmary last week. That is what you really want to talk about, is it not?"

Her rocker sped up, then lost momentum. For someone who'd known her a relatively short period of time, he understood her very well.

He waited patiently for her to put her thoughts into words.

"I . . ." She faltered, then began again, the extent of her misery catching her off guard. "I know you asked Uncle Artemis for permission to court me in order to save my reputation after our . . . our . . ."

"Our kiss," he finished for her.

"Yes," she swallowed, "our kiss—and I appreciate it. Don't misunderstand me, but you don't have to go through with it." Why was this so difficult for her? She'd been practicing for days. "In another week or so, we can tell everyone we don't suit one another and have changed our minds. The gossips will have their day, naturally, but will eventually lose interest. No one need be the wiser, and we can go on with our lives as if nothing happened." She waited on pins and needles for Edward's response to her prepared speech.

He drummed his fingers on the rocker's armrest. After a moment, he turned to her and uttered, "No," in a flat voice.

Confused, Mercy blinked. "No, what?"

"No to everything you said."

She sputtered repeatedly before her mouth formed recognizable words. "Does this mean . . . are you . . ."

He found her hand and folded it inside his. "I want to court you, Mercy."

"You do?" It was what her heart most wanted to hear, and what she'd deemed impossible.

"Yes."

"But I thought we'd agreed not to—that you're returning to Canada."

"I had a lot of time to think this week." He stroked the back of her hand with his thumb. "I have a good job here, and I am not sure I want to give it up."

"But what about your daughter?"

"If your uncle can spare me, we will go to Canada and bring Jacqueline back with us."

"We?"

"Would you like that?"

"Oh, Edward!" Mercy planted her feet firmly on the porch floor, afraid that any second she might start floating on air.

"Then you are agreeable?" His smile showed his pleasure.

"Yes, I'm agreeable."

He reached over and pulled her to him for a quick, but toe-tingling kiss. Only the fear of Sara Jane catching them prevented Mercy from throwing herself at her brand new intended.

The next hour flew by in a whirlwind. Mort Carmichael insisted on walking home, so the Ketchems gave Edward a lift in their Model T Ford. His parting to Mercy was a chaste peck on the cheek for the benefit of her overprotective uncle, and a whispered promise of more to come.

She couldn't touch a bite of the cold supper her aunt laid out later that evening and attempted to mend some clothes instead. After pricking herself in the thumb a half-dozen times, she gave up and let herself daydream about Edward and the sections in Sara Jane's mail order catalogues with wedding dresses.

Before retiring, she decided to read some of her father's journal, specifically the passages where he wrote about her mother. Those had always held special meaning for her, especially after today.

She opened the drawer in her night stand, which held the journal, and reached inside. Her hand came away empty. Fighting panic, she pulled the drawer completely open. It was empty, except for an unfinished letter to an old friend from boarding school.

In a mad rush, Mercy tore about the room. Her frantic search bore no results. Out in the hall, she pounded on her aunt and uncle's bedroom door. They hadn't seen the journal outside Mercy's bedroom for months, but willingly helped her search the rest of the house, to no avail.

With sagging shoulders, Mercy went back to her room, sat on the bed, and burst into tears. Her father's journal was missing. *Who*, she asked herself, *would have taken it? And why*?

* * *

The whistle blew, signaling the noon lunch break. Edward crouched down and sat with his back against the tunnel's stone wall, stretching out his leg. It still hurt him, but only off and on.

He fumbled in his lunch pail for the *tamales* Luiz had packed. The boy had ridden Samson to the Mexican town of *Rio Concho* the day before and returned with a supply of food unlike any Edward had ever seen. He didn't much care for the cornmeal stuffed with spicy meat, but his hunger won out, and he finished the *tamales* in a few quick bites.

The light in the lower levels of the mine was hardly enough to eat by, much less read. Nonetheless, he took out the letter he'd received from his brother, Rene, in the morning's post. Carefully, he unfolded the drawing which his brother had included with the letter. The other miners' friendly chatter faded into the background as he studied his daughter's handiwork. A stick-figure man in an oversized hat stood next to a misshapen tree—Jacqueline's concept of a cactus from what Rene had written.

"Whatcha got?" Thomas asked, leaning over.

"My daughter drew this for me."

"Daughter?" Thomas snorted. "You're jokin'."

"No, I am not." Edward pointed to the top of the drawing where *Papa* was scrawled in childish handwriting.

"Well, I'll be." Thomas slapped his thigh. "Edward Cartier's got himself a kid. Who'd've thought a ladies' man like you would ever tie the knot."

"Don't believe everything you hear, Thomas."

The other man raised an eyebrow. "About you being a ladies' man, or tying the knot?"

"Both."

Thomas shook his head in disbelief. "Ain't you just full of surprises today."

"Hey, Carpenter. You in or not?" One of the other miners

waved Thomas over to join him and his buddies in a card game.

"I'm in, I'm in. Hold your horses." His interest elsewhere, Thomas stomped to his feet and left Edward alone to continue reading Rene's letter.

Edward had trouble picturing the little boy who'd faced the wall more often than he'd faced the catechism teacher as a man of the cloth, but the town's people adored the reformed troublemaker and wholeheartedly accepted him as their spiritual leader. Edward didn't begrudge his brother staying behind while he'd left. They each had a job to do and a place to do it.

He set Jacqueline's drawing atop his lunch pail and opened Rene's letter. Skipping the first page, which he'd already read, he went straight to the second page and the paragraphs which worried him the most.

You have been so good to us, dear brother. I hate asking for one more favor, but I must. Our father, as you know, is greatly troubled by his rheumatism. There are days when he cannot get out of bed. Jean has taken over care of the ewes. It is all he can manage and still attend school. He has offered to quit and assume more of our father's responsibilities on the farm. At twelve, he does not think he needs an education. I will not allow this to happen, and I am sure you support my position.

There is, however, the unfortunate problem of having enough grain to feed the ewes through winter, and seed for the spring planting. With God's blessing, the ewes will deliver a flock of healthy lambs and our crops will flourish, ending this time of terrible woe for good. If it is at all possible, could you send another two hundred dollars? That should be enough to carry us through. If you are not able, we will understand. But we pray that you can.

* * *

Another two hundred dollars.

Artemis Bidwell had promised to pay Edward half that amount for protecting Mercy on her prospecting trips into the mountains. He'd promised another hundred dollars if Edward discouraged her from going altogether.

The spicy *tamales* churned uncomfortably in his stomach.

Protecting Mercy was easy. The same couldn't be said for discouraging her. Since her father's journal disappeared last Sunday after dinner with the Ketchems, she was more determined than ever to find the mine. Already she'd arranged another trip to the *Mano del Diablo* Mountains for the coming Saturday. She believed they were closing in on the mine's location and that someone wanted to beat them to it. If she was right, it would explain a number of things; including the disappearing journal, the vandalism of the wagon, and the mysterious rider Edward had spotted their first trip out.

Who was behind it all? He'd asked himself the same question over and over, and had yet to come up with a likely suspect. Mort Carmichael often sprang to his mind, but other than a dislike of Edward and a few odd coincidences, there was nothing concrete tying Mort to the Silver Angel Mine.

Putting his brother's letter together with Jacqueline's drawing, Edward returned both to his shirt front pocket. Even if he could discourage Mercy, he wasn't sure he wanted to. Somewhere along the way he'd become embroiled in her quest, and felt compelled to see it through—for himself as well as her, Frosty, and Luiz.

It was an admirable ambition, but one which placed him squarely between a rock and a hard spot. His family needed money and Artemis Bidwell provided the most readily available means. In order to obtain the money, however, Edward had to convince the woman he was considering marrying to abandon her cherished dream.

It was not an easy choice.

He involuntarily clenched a fist and pounded the hard tunnel floor. There had to be another solution, one that enabled him to obtain the money without forcing Mercy into something she didn't want. How he'd manage it eluded him, but manage it he would. Even if he had to mill it himself, the Cartier family would have their grain for the ewes and seed for spring. And Jean would stay in school.

More than anything, Edward wanted to return home—at the very least for a visit. He laid his head back against the stone wall and closed his eyes. Having buried his emotions for so long, the sudden rush of homesickness overwhelmed him.

What would his family say if he did arrive for Christmas? What would they say if he arrived with Mercy, his new bride? How would Jacquline feel? She'd never known her mother. Anne-Marie died when their daughter was an infant. For that matter, she hardly knew Edward. She'd been raised these last two years by Edward's sister and brother-in-law, and undoubtedly considered them her parents.

"Cartier? You here?" A miner the men had nicknamed Pony entered the tunnel, ducking to avoid hitting his head on the wooden beam supporting the opening.

"Yes. What is it?" Edward struggled to stand.

"Mr. Bidwell sent me," Pony said. "He's up top and wants to see you right away."

"Thank you." Edward set his lunch pail in a corner, sending a clear message of his intention to return. Since news of his courtship with the mine superintendent's niece spread, he'd been the target of considerable ribbing. Mort Carmichael was the worst offender, accusing Edward of receiving special treatment.

Ten pairs of eyes trailed him and Pony down the dimly lit tunnel. Small talk came to a grinding halt. Edward ignored them. He had no idea why Artemis Bidwell wanted to see him, but he'd bet the two hundred dollars his family needed that it wasn't for any special treatment. He may one day be the mine superintendent's nephew-in-law, but that didn't cut him any slack when it came to work.

Riding the cage up and down the shafts was Edward's least favorite part of the job. It rattled and shook with each foot he and Pony ascended. Edward didn't look down. Dozens of miners died or were seriously injured each year from falls. In a bizarre and tragic accident the previous year, a miner was killed when a large dog somehow found its way into the mine and slipped from the cage. The animal fell two hundred feet before landing on the unsuspecting miner. The memory of the man's broken and mangled body still gave Edward the shakes.

Artemis Bidwell met them at the top. "Come with me, Edward," he said without preamble, and led the way down the main tunnel toward the outside.

It was, Edward noted, the first time the mine superintendent had called him by his given name. Did that bode good, or ill, tidings? He'd learn soon enough. Once outside, they hiked a gravel walkway to a high spot where three stone benches were arranged in a semi-circle. Thatcher Newlin, owner of the Paradise Consolidated Copper Company, had the area cleared so visiting dignitaries could enjoy a bird's-eye view of the entire mining operation.

Sitting on the middle bench, Artemis Bidwell motioned for Edward to take the one beside him. He extracted a handkerchief from his pocket and mopped his brow. "I'd like to speak to you about Mercy."

Edward nodded. He'd been anticipating such a talk since that day in the infirmary. But after reading Rene's letter, he felt less prepared to deal with it.

"You haven't been keeping your end of the bargain," Artemis Bidwell stated, his voice gruff.

"Sir?"

"You and I have an agreement. In addition to protecting Mercy, you were supposed to discourage her. You've gone above and beyond with the first part," he stared pointedly at Edward's leg, "but have fallen mighty short on the second."

"I have been waiting for an opportunity." Avoiding making a decision was more accurate, but Edward admitted that only to himself.

"Waiting, my foot! You need to *make* an opportunity. She's planning another prospecting trip this Saturday. I want it to be her last one. Trick her if you have to."

The suggestion didn't set well with Edward. He was bothered enough already by keeping the terms of his agreement with Artemis Bidwell from Mercy, and didn't want to add to it. "I admit I am not convinced the mine exists, and the risk of danger is great. But those are not reasons enough for me to be dishonest. Finding the mine is important to her."

"Yes, yes, yes," the older man grumbled impatiently. It's important to her, but it's also a complete waste of time. The mine is a myth. It doesn't exist. You need to lay down the law, Edward."

"I am not sure I am in a position to, as you say, lay down the law."

"You're going to marry her, aren't you? If memory serves me, you stated your intentions were honorable. Has that changed?"

"The purpose of courtship is to determine if we are a good match. If it turns out we are, then we will marry, assuming she'll have me."

"Do you love her?"

"I . . ." Did he? He cared about her. Very much. And he was attracted to her. At night, when he lay in bed, he envisioned sharing that same bed with Mercy. He'd met many pretty women in the years since his late wife's death. None had evoked such yearnings in him except Mercy. But was that love, or another, less noble, emotion? "I have feelings for your niece, sir. I believe those feelings will grow into love."

Artemis Bidwell grunted. "I have only sons. What I know about these things doesn't amount to a hill of beans. But from the way Mercy's acting, my guess is she's in love with you, or thinks she is." His tone hardened. "I don't want her hurt. Not by you, and not by the mine."

"I understand."

"Do you?" He leaned forward, resting his forearms on his knees and rubbing his hands together. "I worry about her. My brother lost his life. I refuse to let the same fate befall her."

For the first time, Edward questioned just how far his boss would go to safeguard Mercy. Would he, for instance, steal her father's journal or vandalize the wagon in an attempt to deter her?

"I will protect her. You have my solemn promise on that."

"Then having a wife who spends her days treasure hunting instead of keeping your home and raising your children is acceptable to you?"

Edward had the distinct impression he was being tested. As such, he spoke his mind, but was careful to keep his temper in check. "That is a matter for Mercy and I to decide, not for you to dictate."

The older man laughed agreeably, surprising Edward.

"No, I guess it isn't." He took out his handkerchief and mopped his brow again. "I like you, Edward. You're one of the few men in Paradise who's not afraid to stand up to me. And if you do eventually marry my niece, you'll probably be standing up to me a lot." A smile accompanied the friendly threat.

Edward returned with his own friendly threat, "Let us hope not."

The two men briefly took stock of one another. Apparently satisfied with where they stood, Artemis Bidwell asked, "I suppose you heard about Cal O'Donnell?"

"Yes," Edward answered, wondering what his coworker's firing the previous morning had to do with anything.

"Old man Newlin wants that new tunnel opened up by the end of the month. There are overseas orders stacked two feet high on his desk and he'll do whatever is necessary to fill them. O'Donnell wasn't getting the job done." The mine superintendent appraised Edward through narrowed eyes. "Think you can?"

"A promotion?"

"And a hefty bonus if your crew opens the tunnel by the deadline."

Edward's heart beat faster. Here was the solution to his money dilemma, one that didn't involve Mercy and the mine. His mouth curved up in a confident smile. "I can do it."

"Good. Then the job's yours." Artemis Bidwell sobered, all evidence of his earlier good humor vanished. "On one condition."

Edward's speeding heart slowed. He should have seen this coming, but he'd let his excitement about the promotion cloud his thinking. "Talk Mercy out of searching for the mine," he finished dully.

"That's right."

He took a deep breath. "I do not know if such a thing is possible. She will not listen to reason."

"Like her father before her. Don't think I haven't heard what folks are saying about her, and I don't like it."

"Nor do I," Edward concurred.

Mercy's inquiries around town concerning the missing journal had stirred the gossips, who were comparing her to her late father and his obsession with the mine. Unflattering names were being bandied about, and Edward could understand her uncle's concern, having been the subject of many rumors himself.

"Then do something about it! Now that you and Mercy are courting, you going with her on these trips only gives the gossips that much more to talk about."

"You asked me to go."

"Yes, in order to discourage her," Artemis Bidwell snapped, "which you haven't done."

"You are right." Edward wanted to argue, but couldn't.

"Convince Mercy to stay home, Edward, and the job is yours." Artemis Bidwell drove his point home. "You'll need the extra money if the two of you decide to marry."

His boss didn't know the half of it.

What seemed merely confusing a little earlier had now become complicated. Edward needed to put some distance between himself and the situation.

"I will think about it."

"No time. I need a decision today. Old man Newlin has a deadline. If you don't take the job, I'm going to give it to someone else."

Edward fingered the papers in his pocket; Rene's letter and Jacqueline's drawing. He thought of Mercy. Being the talk of Paradise—which he'd unwittingly contributed to—might be the least of her problems. If her suspicions about her father's death were true, her life could be in serious danger. Someone with malicious intentions had an interest in the mine, and there was no telling where they'd draw the line.

He'd promised her uncle he'd protect her. What if convincing her to give up searching for the mine *was* the best way to accomplish that? He'd be a sorry husband if he didn't take care of his wife, and a sorry father if he didn't provide for his daughter.

"All right." He extended his hand. "I'll take the job."

Artemis Bidwell beamed as he clasped Edward's hand and shook it vigorously. "You made the right decision."

Had he? Why did he feel so unsure?

Chapter Nine

We made our monthly trip into Paradise today for supplies. To my delight, when I checked with the post-master, there was a letter from Mercy waiting for me. My delight quickly turned to concern when I read it.

She's talking again about coming out here to live with me. I don't know why she wants to leave Boston. Not only are the people and land more civilized there, she also has a good position at the school, one that pays well. Her mother would be so proud of her.

I think my daughter has spent too much time reading those absurd dime novels. Nothing portrayed in them is close to accurate. She has this romantic notion in her head that she can join me in my search for the mine and together we will have a grand and glorious adventure.

While I admit there is a certain appeal to having Mercy here with me, I don't dare encourage her. The life

125

I have chosen for myself is a hard and dangerous one.
One I want my only child to stay far, far away from.
                                    Charles Oliver Bidwell

"Look, there's Frosty and Buttercup," Mercy shouted as she guided Samson through an opening in the scrub brush.

Edward followed the wagon, riding the bay mare. The wagon bumped sharply when the right front wheel sunk into a hole, throwing Mercy and Luiz off balance.

Once they were safely in the clearing, Edward turned his attention to the mountainside and watched Frosty pick his way down a steep incline. The old prospector was easy to spot, his red-checkered shirt a bright contrast to the muted browns and greens of the desert. Buttercup ambled along behind him, daintily stepping over obstacles in her path.

A hundred feet over their heads, the rock wings jutted skyward. There was never a question they would return to this place to resume their search. Mercy's convictions remained strong and unwavering; the Silver Angel Mine existed, and it was somewhere in the vicinity of the rock wings.

They all reached the sparse campsite within minutes of each other. Wisps of lingering smoke drifted up from the small fire Frosty had built hours earlier to cook his breakfast. He grabbed Samson's bridle and held the mule while Mercy and Luiz crawled down from the wagon, both of them full of excited chatter. Edward dismounted and tied his horse's reins to the side of the wagon, then reached in and began unloading the tools and equipment they'd brought.

"Luiz," he called to the boy. "Give me a hand."

Mercy was busy ridding herself of trail dust, her hands brushing the front of her full skirt. Around her waist she wore a thick leather belt with a square metal buckle. The simple work outfit accentuated her womanly shape, and Edward's body involuntarily responded.

Beneath her straw hat, her face was aglow with anticipation. "I can't wait to get started. It's still early, do you mind waiting a bit for lunch?"

"No, I am not hungry—but Luiz may have a different opinion."

His helper nodded vigorously.

She laughed gaily, and Edward forced himself to smile. Eating was the farthest thing from his mind. He'd been in a quandary the past few days, ever since his meeting with Artemis Bidwell. Having accepted the promotion, Edward was now obligated to fulfill his end of the agreement. Worry that he was doing the right thing, combined with concern for his family, robbed him not only of his appetite, but of sleep as well.

Sometime that morning in the small hours before dawn, he'd awoke with a start from an from a disturbing dream. In it, he relived Anne-Marie's death and the consuming guilt he'd experienced at not being able to save her. Then, before his eyes, Anne-Marie changed into Mercy. Edward came abruptly awake, agonized at the thought of losing Mercy like he had his late wife, and vowing to prevent history from repeating itself.

Feeling more positive about his agreement with Artemis Bidwell, he set about devising a means of convincing Mercy to forego her search for the Silver Angel Mine. While getting dressed, an idea came to him. The more he rolled it over in his tired mind, the more certain he was he'd found the perfect solution. If he played his cards just right, said exactly the right thing, he'd be able to obtain the money his family needed, satisfy his boss, and please Mercy all in one shot.

The only trickery involved would be catching his future bride alone during the next two days to speak with her in private.

He glanced up from his task to see Frosty leading Buttercup to the wagon. While he and Luiz loaded the donkey's packsaddle with what they'd need for the afternoon, the old prospector unharnessed Samson and unsaddled the mare. He then secured the animals in a small makeshift pen he'd built during the two weeks since their previous trip to the rock wings.

"Take these." Edward handed a candle and several matches to Mercy. "Put them in your pocket."

She complied without asking why. Any miner worth his salt always carried a candle and matches with him—or *her* in this instance.

Edward pocketed his own candle and matches. Having fed and watered the animals, Frosty returned to help Edward finish tying the pack saddles.

"Come along." Mercy ruffled Luiz's jet black hair, which had recently been trimmed. "Let's get lunch ready. What do you say?"

"*Sí, sí, Senorita* Bidwell." He patted his stomach and licked his lips. "*Tengo mucho hambre.*"

During a quick meal of soda crackers, canned tomatoes, and dried beef, they discussed where to start. Frosty had spent the last two weeks camped out at the rock wings and had the most input. According to him, the deeply rutted summit showed great potential.

"For what it's worth, the ground here abouts is the right color. Kinda hard gettin' up to them wings, though. Awful steep near the top."

"Perhaps we should split into pairs in order to cover a larger area." Edward strived to sound casual and not like he had an ulterior motive. "Mercy and I could take the far side. You and Luiz, the near side." He directed his remark to Frosty.

The veteran prospector chewed thoughtfully on a piece of

dried beef. "Ain't much on the near side. I've been over nearly every inch. The way I figure it, if we all work the far side, we'll get to most of it in the two days before y'all have to head back to Paradise."

Edward bit back his frustration. "That makes sense, *mon ami*. We will stick together." There was always tonight to talk with Mercy. He'd suggest a stroll after supper.

"I agree with Edward," Mercy chimed in. "I think we should split into pairs. We can each start on one end and work toward the center."

Frosty lifted one shoulder in an indifferent shrug. "We could do that if you want."

Relief washed over Edward, and he smiled at Mercy. He'd have his chance to speak with her after all.

"I want to go with you," Luiz said to Edward through a mouth full of food. "You are my partner, no? That is what you call me at home. Your little partner."

The boy's crestfallen expression pulled at Edward, and he relented. He'd grown very fond of his charge and didn't like disappointing him. "Yes, you are my little partner. Of course you will go with me."

Luiz beamed.

The light of approval shining in Mercy's eyes made the change in Edward's plans worthwhile. Surely an opportunity would present itself over the next two days. He need only curb his impatience until then.

Edward stood, stretched his back, and surveyed the ridge. To his right, about twenty yards away, Frosty knelt on a narrow ledge, balancing himself on one knee. Using a hand pick, the older man chipped away at a jagged rock protruding from the ledge. As he did, small pieces of debris broke loose and tumbled downward in a miniature avalanche.

Mercy's late father, Charles Oliver Bidwell, believed the

Indians hid the entrance to the mine after the revolt which ended in the deaths of the Jesuit Priests. Assuming he was right, they'd chosen to concentrate their search, not on obvious apertures in the mountainside, but rather on rock clusters and boulders substantial enough to obscure a man-sized hole.

The work was strenuous, meticulous, and painstakingly slow. Edward and Frosty were used to it. Mercy wasn't. To her credit, she'd not complained once, nor had she given anything less than her best effort.

She would feel it tomorrow, however. When Edward last checked on her an hour ago, her hands were scraped and bleeding, the palms blistered, and the backs sunburned. He thought to bring along a pair of leather gloves on their next excursion, then remembered that if all went well, this excursion would be their last.

Though she didn't admit it, he knew her knees were rubbed raw and her muscles were crying out for rest. A night sleeping on the hard ground would only increase her misery.

Shielding his eyes, he scanned the ridge to his left and found her. She appeared to be clearing dead shrubs and branches from a shallow hole of some kind. It was difficult for him to tell, as the setting sun cast her in dark shadows.

"How much longer?" Luiz sat on the ground not far from Edward, his arms locked around his bent knees. Every once in a while he'd toss a small pebble down the side of the ridge, scaring some hapless dove or quail into flight. "I am hungry."

Edward didn't doubt that. The boy could out-eat two grown men, but he suspected Luiz's whining stemmed more from boredom and fatigue than actual hunger. Luiz had lost interest in helping about mid-afternoon. Edward was reluctant to let the boy go off by himself and play after what happened with the rattlesnakes, and insisted he stick nearby.

With each passing minute, Luiz became more and more restless.

"It will be dark soon." Edward removed his hat and slapped it on his thigh, dislodging a thick layer of dust and dirt. After combing his fingers through his sweat-dampened hair, he replaced the hat and adjusted it to a more comfortable fit. "I suppose we can quit for now."

Luiz let out a whoop and jumped to his feet, suddenly bursting with energy.

"*Mon ami*," Edward hollered to Frosty through cupped hands. "Are you ready to call it a day?" A quick glance over his shoulder confirmed Mercy had heard him and stopped working in order to listen.

"There's another hour of daylight left," Frosty hollered back. "Hate to waste it."

Edward had to agree, but he was also worried about Mercy and didn't think she could last much longer. He turned toward her and again cupped his hands around his mouth. "Mercy, why don't you and Luiz return to camp and start supper? Frosty and I will stay here and keep working."

Even from a distance, he could discern the deliberation in her face. She didn't want to quit unless the rest of them did. Exhaustion apparently prevailed, for she struggled to her feet and waved, then bent to pick up her tools.

"Go help her," Edward told Luiz, who immediately scurried off, glad for any excuse to hurry supper along. "And watch yourself."

Edward returned to his task of digging, but kept one eye on Mercy and Luiz. They weren't particularly high up, but the ridge sloped at an almost vertical angle in some places.

A scuffling sound ricocheted off the mountain walls. Edward's head whipped around to see Luiz bounding back up the ridge to a fallen Mercy. The load of tools he carried dropped from his arms.

"*Senorita* Bidwell!"

With a loud clatter, Edward's shovel hit the ground. He ran to Mercy as fast as he could, his boots slipping and sliding on the loose gravel. By the time he reached her, his breath came in ragged bursts.

"Are you hurt, *chère?*" He kneeled beside her, elbowing Luiz out of the way.

She tried to move, and winced. "Oh, Edward. It's hard to tell. I ache everywhere." The wince became a feeble smile. "I feel so stupid. One second I was walking, then the next thing I know, I'm flat on my back."

"Can you get up?"

"I think so." She succeeded in standing, but not without a struggle.

"I'll carry you the rest of the way."

"Don't be ridiculous." She batted his hands away. "I can make it."

The remaining descent proved tedious. Mercy frequently bit her bottom lip to stifle a cry. Her injuries appeared to be minor bumps and bruises for the most part, but added to her array of existing afflictions, she was in sad shape.

Edward had sent Luiz ahead with Mercy's tools, and the boy met them in camp. His large, brown eyes were filled with concern.

"Will the *senorita* be all right?"

"I'm fine," she assured him.

"You go fetch my tools now and bring them back." Edward hitched his chin in the direction of the ridge. "Then help Frosty."

Luiz frowned. "But what about supper?"

"Go," Edward said sternly. "We will worry about supper when you return."

He settled a grateful Mercy on the wagon seat, which had been placed on the ground shortly after their arrival. While she removed her hat and rested, he stirred the fire, added kindling, and put on a kettle of water to heat. When he returned from locating the bandages and a tin of ointment they'd brought along, steam poured from the kettle's spout. He laid a clean wash rag in the bottom of a chipped porcelain bowl and poured hot water over it.

"That's a peculiar way to fix coffee," Mercy said from where she sat.

"I am not fixing coffee." He started for her.

She got a nervous look on her face. "Tell me this isn't going to hurt."

"And have you call me a liar?"

"I was afraid of that." She laid her head back, closed her eyes and tucked her hands under her arms.

"But I can tell you it will be over soon. And then you will feel much better."

She cracked one eye. "Promise?"

"*Oui.*" Crouching in front of her, he set the bowl, ointment, and bandages on the seat beside her. "I promise." He held out his hand, and she reluctantly placed one of hers in it. Gently, he examined the blistered and bleeding flesh.

"Ouch!" She flinched.

He clucked like a mother hen as he squeezed excess water from the wash rag and began cleaning her hand. "You should have said something. There was no need for this."

"You, Frosty, and I are in this together. It's not fair for you and him to do all the work."

"We are stronger and have more experience."

"I'll get stronger, and I can learn. You'll see. I'll do much better next time."

Edward swallowed. Here was the opening he needed. "What if there is no next time?"

"I beg your pardon?"

He began washing her other hand. "Prospecting is difficult work. This is our third trip into the mountains and on each occasion we have met with trouble."

"I didn't expect it to be easy."

"But did you expect to hurt yourself? Or almost drown in the river? In a hundred years I did not imagine your uncle would shoot me."

"Are you saying we should give up searching for the mine?"

Using the task of applying ointment as an excuse not to meet her flashing green eyes, he said, "No, but what if we postponed it for a while?"

"Postpone it?" She drew back, clearly startled by his suggestion. "Why?"

"You are hurt and will need time to recover."

"A week. Two at the most.

"Look at yourself. How will you operate the switchboard and that typewriting machine at the office on Monday?" He tenderly wrapped her left hand in a bandage. "You could barely remove your hat a minute ago."

"I'll figure something out."

"And your uncle? What will he say when his secretary cannot perform her duties?"

"I *said* I'll figure something out."

"*Chère*." Edward gentled his voice as he knotted the first bandage and started on her other hand. "If we are to be in Quebec for Christmas, we will have to leave Paradise the first week in December."

"What difference does that make? There are plenty of Saturdays between now and December."

He smiled at her. "Which Saturday between now and December will you pick for your wedding day?"

Her eyes widened.

"We cannot travel to Quebec without marrying first, and planning a wedding takes time. It is already September."

"Are you sure?" she asked in a half-whisper. "I thought

we agreed to wait until we got to know each other better."

He cupped her dirt-smudged cheek and stroked it with the pad of his thumb. "Yes, I am sure, and we will have the rest of our lives to get to know each other better."

Maybe it had happened when he woke that morning from his terrible nightmare. Or when he'd seen her on her knees, clearing a hole of debris until her once smooth hands were bloodied. It could have been when she and Luiz fixed lunch together, the two of them laughing and carrying on like old friends. The exact moment was irrelevant. All Edward knew was that sometime during the day he realized what a rare and remarkable woman Mercy was, and what a fool he'd be not to make her his wife.

"Aunt Connie will help with the wedding." She leaned her cheek into his palm.

"As you say here, wild horses could not keep her away."

"Planning a wedding won't take all that much time. We can easily fit in one or two more prospecting trips."

"What about traveling clothes? Every bride should have a new wardrobe. And new furniture for the house? I have been a bachelor for many years and do not own much that is suitable for a wife."

"I don't care about that." She removed his hand from her cheek and squeezed it. "Your house is fine. A few pictures and some curtains will make a world of difference."

"Nonsense. We can go shopping in Phoenix. You aunt will accompany us, naturally."

"Honestly, Edward." She laughed brightly. "I'm used to very little. Remember, I grew up in boarding school where I was allowed only the barest necessities. Your family needs your money more than I do. Send it to them. Besides, we're sure to receive all sorts of lovely wedding presents."

"It will give me pleasure to buy nice things for you. Jacqueline, too. She is a big girl now and should have her own bed. Some toys, too, I think. She has been through so much, and I want her to be happy living here with us."

"She will be." Mercy squeezed his hand again. "I can't wait to meet her."

"It is agreed then? No more prospecting?"

"Agreed."

Edward relaxed, the tension of the last few days flowing out of him in a rush. Everything was going to work out fine after all. He rose and helped Mercy up.

She tugged clumsily on her twisted skirt, then grinned at him. "Until we return from Canada. Then, we can resume searching." She scanned the campsite. "Where's Luiz? I'm suddenly starving."

He was slow to respond, having assumed Mercy would be too preoccupied with wedding and travel plans to give the mine another thought. He should have known better. "Ah . . . about that, it might be difficult to get away once we return."

She turned to face him, a small crease in her brow. "Why?"

"Well . . . there is Jacqueline. What will we do with her while we are prospecting?"

"Bring her along."

"She is too young. I would worry about her getting lost or hurt."

"Aunt Connie will watch her for us. She loves children."

"I hate the idea of leaving her behind every weekend after being separated from her for so long."

"I understand." Mercy's features softened, but she didn't relent. "Don't fret. We'll think of something."

Edward mentally grasped for straws. If he didn't succeed in distracting Mercy, there was no telling how her uncle would react. Artemis Bidwell had been adamant that this be their last trip into the mountains. He might give Edward's promotion to someone else. Then how would he obtain the money his family needed, or support a wife and child? He had to think. What, more than anything else, would persuade Mercy to give up prospecting?

"And if you . . . if we . . . should have a baby? What then?"

"Oh!" Her cheeks and neck flushed bright red.

"It is possible," he continued, sensing he'd hit upon the right strategy. "And if you become . . . with child, I would insist you stay home, for your sake and the baby's."

"Well, that hasn't happened yet," she said airily, obviously embarrassed by the personal nature of their conversation. "And may not happen for a long while. Who knows?"

"You do not want children?"

"Of course I want children," she said defensively.

"What if we have a family and never find the mine?"

"I don't know, Edward." She swung away from him. "Why the sudden questions?"

He came up behind her and placed his hands on her shoulders. "I am just considering all the possibilities."

"Are you? It seems to me you're coming up with one reason after another why we should give up searching for the mine."

"Would that be so awful?" He bent down and pressed a kiss to the top of her head. "Then I could spend all my days off with you and Jacqueline, the two beautiful ladies in my life."

She curled against him. "It's only that I've dreamed of finding the Silver Angel Mine for years and years, ever since my father first began telling me stories about it in his letters. I'd always hoped he and I would find it together." Her voice cracked. "I'd be almost as happy if you and I found it."

Her poignant outpouring had the same effect as a sucker

punch to the gut. Edward stepped away, requiring a moment to recuperate. What a heel he'd been, trying his best to take away her cherished dream in order to serve his own purpose. She deserved much better than that.

She deserved the truth.

With sudden insight, Edward understood the best course of action was—and had always been—not to distract Mercy, but to be honest with her. From the moment they'd decided to court, he should have informed her of the full terms of his agreement with her uncle. They could have discussed the matter and made any decisions jointly, as married couples were supposed to.

Well, better late than never.

"Mercy."

"Yes, Edward." She smiled expectantly.

"There is something I have to tell you. Something I should have told you weeks ago."

Her smile faltered. "What is it?"

"Your uncle and I have an agreement."

"I know about that."

"No." He spoke slowly. "We have another agreement. One which you do not know about."

"Another agreement?" She reached for the silver ring she wore around her neck and fingered it through her bandages. "What kind of agreement?"

"Your uncle offered me a promotion. Second shift foreman on level one."

"He did? That's wonderful."

"There is more. The job comes with a condition."

Something in his demeanor set her nerves on edge. "What's the condition?"

"That I convince you to give up searching for the mine."

"I see." She pushed the words through gritted teeth, unprepared for the force of how deeply Edward's confession hurt her. He and her uncle, the two men she cared most about in the world next to her late father, had conspired together behind her back.

"You are upset."

"Yes, I'm upset!" The hurt she felt quickly took the form of anger. Holding her injured hands to her middle, she began pacing. "I can believe Uncle Artemis would do such a thing. He's tried manipulating me in the past. But you!" She stopped to catch her breath. "We are going to be married. How could you?"

"I cannot, *chère*. Which is why I told you."

An awful thought suddenly came to her, leaving a wave of nausea in its wake. "Your proposal. Was it sincere? Or was it part of . . . the *condition*?"

"No." Edward shoved his hat back on his head, his frustration obviously escalating. "Never that."

"Yet it conveniently fits in with your and Uncle Artemis's agreement. Don't you agree?"

"Yes . . . no. It's not what—"

"Enough!" Mercy couldn't bear hearing more of his excuses and stumbled toward the wagon. The ground in front of her blurred as tears filled her eyes.

Edward caught up with her and tugged on her arm. "Listen to me. Please. That is not how it happened."

She attempted to shake off his grip, but her muscles were too sore and weak. "You just said—"

"I asked permission to court you long before your uncle offered me the promotion."

"But not before you entered into an agreement with him," she answered miserably, still not looking at him.

He sighed. "I received a letter from my brother, Rene, this week. Our father is sick, the ewes are without grain, and our youngest brother wants to quit school to work the farm. The promotion and bonus your uncle promised would enable me to send them the two hundred dollars they need to get through the winter. I must take care of them." The tension in his voice revealed the magnitude of his emotions. "And Jacqueline."

"I'm sorry about your family. And I appreciate your obligation to them. It was grossly unfair of Uncle Artemis to put you in the position he did and I will definitely give him a piece of my mind." Her uncle's underhandedness angered her. Edward's cut her to the quick. "But did you have to trick me with a pretend marriage proposal?"

"My proposal was sincere." He was so close to her, his breath tickled the fine hairs on the back of her neck. "You must believe me. I never wanted to hurt you."

She swallowed and pulled away from him. "But you did."

He let her go without any resistance. "I could not stand the thought of losing you, too."

"You wouldn't have lost me, Edward."

"Can you be sure? Look what happened to your father. Someone else is after the mine." He lifted his gaze to the rock wings. "I admit I should not have accepted your uncle's offer, but my intentions were good."

"That doesn't excuse what you did."

"It could if you let it."

"It's not that simple."

"Why? Because you refuse to give up searching for the mine? Even for us and the life we could have together?"

"Don't be ridiculous."

"You have never been rational when it comes to the Silver Angel Mine."

"Just like my father, right?" She stared accusingly at him. "He wasn't rational, cither."

"Finding the mine will not bring him back."

"No. But it will prove . . . it will prove . . ."

"Prove what? Tell me," he said when she continued to hesitate.

The words tore from her and with them, a piece of her heart. "Prove that he shouldn't have left me behind all those years in school."

"I am so sorry, *chère*."

"Why, Edward?" Long suppressed anger rose to the surface. "Why did he do that?"

"He thought he was doing the right thing. A life prospecting in the mountains is not a good one for a young girl."

"The right thing? Ha!" She gave a disgusted shake of her head. "Of course you would defend him. You left your daughter behind, too."

Her barb hit its mark, and he jerked as if slapped. "It is not the same."

She ignored the small voice inside her head reminding her that Edward wasn't her father. They were two different men, but the similarities staggered her. Both had lost their wives. Both had abandoned their daughters and homes. And most importantly, both had put their own wants and needs ahead of her.

Protect her? Care for her? Hardly. She was sick and tired of men running her life, and of men ruining her life; her father, Uncle Artemis, and Edward. They'd all three disappointed her, especially Edward. If he truly loved her, he wouldn't have done what he did. How could she have ever considered marrying him?

"It's good we found out now, before making a horrible mistake," she said, her snippiness masking her heartache.

"Found out what?"

"That we aren't a good match."

"Mercy. We are having an argument. People do that. Even married people. It is no reason to call off the wedding."

"An argument?" How incredibly obtuse of him. "This is much more serious than that."

"You are overreacting."

"With good reason, I'd say."

He grunted his irritation. "I cancelled my agreement with your uncle by telling you about it, and I have apologized."

"Yes, you have, but it makes no difference." She stepped away from him.

"Where are you going?"

The withering look she shot him halted him in his tracks. "For a walk."

He didn't come after her, which suited her just fine.

Didn't it?

Sheer force of will kept the sobs at bay until she rounded the far side of the ridge.

Chapter Ten

June 23, 1904

*T*he *Indian revolt against the Jesuit Priest wasn't the only battle to ever take place for ownership of the Silver Angel Mine. The proof of that lies in the many bones scattered across the desert, some of which I have seen with my own eyes.*

I thought Frosty might keel over from heart failure today when, while exploring a small canyon between the first and second fingers, we stumbled upon the skeletal remains of at least three individuals. I'm presuming they were men. From the looks of his skull, one unfortunate fellow took a bullet to the right temple at close range. Not a very pleasant manner in which to die.

Were they white men? Indians, perhaps? Or some other treasure seekers exploring these mountains? They may even have been Mexicans. Young Mr. Houseman told us a story, that night he visited at our campfire, about a prominent Mexican mining family who came to the Mano del Diablo *Mountains searching for the Silver Angel Mine. Supposedly, the Apaches drove them out in a bloody battle that ended with many deaths. Maybe the bodies we found today were those of the Rodriguezes. I don't suppose we'll ever know.*

Gathering as many bones as we could find, we laid them to rest under a cottonwood tree growing near an underground spring. As I shoveled dirt onto their graves, I couldn't help thinking that I hope I don't end up like these men.

Charles Oliver Bidwell

How could she have ever considered marrying Edward Cartier? There were dozens . . . no, *hundreds* of eligible men in Paradise, and she had to fall for him.

The muscles in her tired legs burned as she hurried, her sobs breaking free just as she reached the other side of the ridge. There, in the darkness, she found comfort. Edward, Luiz, and Frosty might be only fifty yards away, but it felt like five-hundred. And the more distance between them, the better.

Without conscious thought of her direction, Mercy found herself on the footpath leading to the rock wings. Clutching the folds of her skirt, she lifted the hem to her knees and trudged ahead. When she reached the small mesa at the top, she sat on the same rock as before—the one where she and Edward had shared the applesauce. The reminder triggered a fresh onslaught of tears, and she wiped them away with her shirt sleeve.

From below, she heard a rustling sound and with it, an overpowering sense of *déjà vu*. She stood and walked slowly to the edge to investigate. It felt like her father's hand was on her shoulder, guiding her ahead of him as he'd done when she was a little girl.

A three-quarter moon rising in the southwestern sky provided enough light for her to see clearly. As before, a fox scurried along the ledge below her, slinking between low shrubs. All of a sudden, it disappeared into the base of the rock wings.

How peculiar, she thought, that twice she should happen up here and see a fox.

The wings, two triangle-shaped boulders as tall as a man, jutted up and outward from a rounded base. The design was ingenious, Mercy mused as she studied it. Truly a miracle of nature.

Unless it *wasn't* nature's creation.

The thought dawned on her with such clarity, it might have been a forgotten memory resurfacing. The rock wings, or at least part of their structure, were man-made.

The only people to ever occupy this area were Indians and Jesuit Priests. Some said the priests hid the mine, others said the Indians did after their revolt against the priests. Whichever theory was true, the fact remained that the rock wings hid the entrance to the Silver Angel Mine. What other explanation could there be? The concept was so simple and perfect. Why hadn't they realized it before?

Excitement built inside Mercy.

Cupping her hands to her mouth, she stopped short before hollering to the others. She had no doubt she'd found the infamous Silver Angel Mine, but they might not share her certainty. Edward's cutting remark about her not being rational when it came to the mine still rang in her ears. She'd get the proof first, then reveal her discovery.

Visually measuring the drop, she determined the distance wasn't so far she couldn't easily jump it. There also appeared to be ample room to land. With a low grunt, she lowered herself to a sitting position midway between the wings and then dangled her legs over the side while gathering her courage.

Pulling a deep breath into her lungs, she pushed off. Pain radiated up her legs when she hit the ground, causing her to wince. She waited for a slight wave of dizziness to pass before looking around to get her bearings.

A small gasp escaped her lips. At close range, the rock wings were even more imposing. The rounded boulder at the base came almost to her waist and was much narrower than it appeared from the ground. A gap of eight or ten inches separated it from the wings. Wide enough for a fox to slip through, but not a person. She lowered her head and peered into the gap. Pitch black darkness stared back at her, and a stale smell invaded her nostrils.

Straightening, she chewed her lower lip and weighed her options. What might her father have done in the same situation? Give up? Never! Call for help? Possibly. More than likely he'd have tried to move the base. Of course, he'd been much stronger than her, and his hands wouldn't have been bandaged. Alerting the others really was the smart choice. She should head back to camp before it got any later. Knowing Edward, he'd come looking for her soon, and she didn't feel much like talking to him at the moment.

Seconds ticked by, becoming minutes. For no purpose other than to vent her disappointment, she braced her foot on the rock base and pushed.

To her astonishment, it moved.

"What the . . ."

She stared at the gap, which had widened by several inches. Then she braced her foot on the rock base again and pushed a second time. It slid more. How could that be?

With fumbling fingers, she reached into her skirt pocket and extracted the candle Edward had given her. She wasted three matches attempting to light it. Shielding the flame, she crouched down to investigate and almost laughed at her susceptibility. It hadn't been any superior strength on her part that enabled her to move the rock base, but rather wooden runners placed beneath it.

The chuckle died in her throat. Here was confirmation that *something* lay behind the rock wings and *someone* had gone to great lengths to hide it. A rush of adrenaline swept through her with the speed and energy of a swarm of bees.

Angling her body, she slid through the opening. The jagged rock wall scraped her back, and fine, powdery dirt fell into her eyes. She blinked the irritation away, not letting it deter her. Cramps seized her legs, but she fought them off, crab-walking until she was far enough into the opening to stand. And stand she did, rising to her full height.

"Oh, my goodness!" Her whisper echoed off the smooth stone walls, the staccato rhythm matching the elevated beat of her heart.

The tunnel's entrance could hold four people with room to spare, and the ceiling was a foot above Mercy's head. She couldn't determine how far back the tunnel went into the mountain with just a candle. They'd need lanterns to properly explore it. What appeared to be primitive mining equipment was stacked against the tunnel wall, though Mercy couldn't tell for certain. The tools were caked with grime and the wooden handles badly rotted.

It suddenly struck her that the fox was nowhere to be seen. Had it escaped down the tunnel? There was no evidence of a den that she could see. Had it even been real, or just a figment of her imagination? Goose bumps erupted on her arms, and she shivered. When had it turned so cold?

Unreasonable fear blossomed inside her. *Leave*, someone shouted. Then again, it might have been her own instincts warning her of danger. Mercy couldn't shake the disturbing premonition that something bad was about to happen.

Her physical aches and pains forgotten, she spun on her heels and practically dove for the opening. Her quick movements extinguished the candle, plunging her into total darkness.

Her foot went into a hole, and she yelped as she went down on all fours, crashing into the tunnel wall. A fiery pain exploded above her forehead as colored lights pulsated in front of her eyes. Sitting back on her calves, she touched the sensitive knot already forming on her scalp and moaned. She was lucky not to have been knocked unconscious. To her vast relief, she still clutched the candle in her other hand.

When the pulsating lights dimmed sufficiently, she reached into her pocket for her last match. She struck it on the stone floor and with a scratchy hiss, it burst to life. Using extreme care, she held the flame to the blackened candlewick and sighed with gratitude when it caught.

Unsure which direction she faced, Mercy lifted the candle. It was then that she realized she knelt on a very tattered and worn cloth of some kind. Scattered about beside the cloth were what resembled broken sticks.

The fear she'd felt earlier exploded into full-blown horror. In a daze, she raised the candle higher and followed the circle of light up until it settled on the gleaming white face of a grinning skeleton.

Blood curdling screams filled the tunnel until Mercy thought she'd go deaf from the noise. It finally penetrated the heavy layers of cotton surrounding her brain that the screams she heard were her own.

The light from three lanterns only marginally lessened the fright Mercy felt when she looked at the skeleton. After an hour in the tunnel, she still couldn't bring herself to view the open-jawed face, and instead focused her attention on the tunnel walls, her own feet, or the crooked crease on the back of Edward's hat.

As she'd predicted, he'd come looking for her and correctly guessed she'd gone to the mesa at the top of the rock wings. He'd been there when he'd heard her screams. It hadn't taken him but a minute to locate her.

She had no idea how long she'd screamed, only that her throat was raw and it hurt to talk. Edward said he'd had to shake her repeatedly to rouse her from her hysterics. She believed him, for Mercy had never been so terrified in all her life.

"Reckon he's one of them priests?" Frosty asked.

"He must be," Edward answered. "See, there's a wooden cross around his middle."

"What was he doing here? Guarding the mine, you suppose?"

"He may have been put here by the Indians as a warning for others to stay away. Or he may have hidden here during the revolt, then become trapped when the Indians blocked the entrance to the mine."

Mercy fiddled with her bandages as she listened to them discuss the skeleton. How long did they plan on staying? Wouldn't it make more sense to return in the morning when they could explore the mine in the light? After Edward had found her and calmed her down, he'd gone back out to the ledge and called to Frosty to join them. No one had suggested she return to camp to recover from her shock. They were apparently too fascinated with the skeleton and the mine to think of that. Not that Mercy could blame them.

Funny, she couldn't recount the number of times she'd imagined finding the mine, but not once in her various scenarios had she included the presence of a guardian skeleton. It dampened the thrill. She should be dancing and shouting with glee instead of subduing a case of the willies.

Yawning, she covered her mouth with her hand. The excitement of the last hour, added to the physically grueling and emotionally draining afternoon, had sapped her remaining strength. Were it not for a most undesirable bed partner, she'd lay down on the tunnel floor and sleep right there. Maybe when she woke up the skeleton would be gone, and they could go about the business of exploring the mine—minus a pair of black, hollow eyes following their every move.

"What is that?" Edward asked, pointing.

Mercy reacted to something in his tone and followed the direction of his finger. To her distress, it lead straight to the skeleton. Her stomach pitched.

"Don't rightly know. Mighty peculiar looking." Frosty squatted beside the skeleton and lifted the tattered cloth, which, two centuries earlier, had been a robe.

Underneath it was a large leather sack, knotted at the end with a drawstring. A religious emblem had been burned into the leather. They'd noticed the same emblem etched in the wall by the entrance to the tunnel. Mercy had also seen it at the mission, carved over the archway leading into the sanctuary.

Frosty picked up the sack and gave it a shake. "Right heavy." He looked up at Edward—who nodded somberly—then untied the drawstring. No one made a sound. Turning the sack over, Frosty poured a portion of the contents into his cupped palm. Sparkling silver coins clinked merrily as they landed.

They all caught their breaths.

"*Mon Dieu*," Edward exclaimed. "It *is* silver."

"Lots of it." Frosty cackled. "A small fortune. Mercy, girl. You did it. You found the mine! And now you're a rich woman."

"Silver," Mercy repeated, still not quite believing what her eyes and ears confirmed. She looked at Frosty and then Edward, expecting them to break into raucous laughter and tell her it was all a prank. They didn't. "If my father had known about the rock wings, he'd have found the mine first."

"Sure as shootin' he would've." Leaping to his feet, Frosty distributed a portion of silver coins to each of them. Mercy and Edward were rendered speechless as they examined their find. The coins were cold to the touch and heavy, Mercy noticed. Like her ring. Though impossible to explain, she instinctively knew both had come from the same place in the Earth and had been formed by the same two hands.

Reality struck her with full force. She had found the mine! They had all found it, each of them contributing in some way. Even the argument with Edward had served a purpose. Without it happening precisely when it did, she would never had been on the mesa to see the fox disappear between the rock wings.

"How much is it worth?" she asked in a reverent whisper. "The silver, I mean. Not the mine."

Frosty shrugged. "Have to take it to the assayer's office to find out for sure."

"But if you were to venture a guess?" she prodded.

He bounced a coin in his hand, then put it in his mouth and bit down. His bushy white eyebrows shot up. "Good quality. I reckon the whole lot'll go for a thousand dollars, maybe two."

Edward gave a low whistle.

"In all my days I ain't never seen so much shiny stuff." The gleam in Frosty's eyes matched the silver coins he held. "And this is just the beginning. We got us a whole boat load of silver to dig out in this place."

"We'll split the claim three ways," Mercy said resolutely. "And a share for Luiz. He helped, too."

"Guess the tyke's entitled to something, seeing as he's the one who knew about the rock wings." Frosty tugged open the sack, and they each replaced their silver coins. "We'd best get to Paradise at the crack of dawn to file the claim. News travels fast in these parts. We'll more than likely have visitors soon, and some of them won't be paying us a social call, if you catch my meaning."

"You and I will stay here," Edward said, "and keep watch. Mercy and Luiz can drive the wagon back to town." He pivoted to face her. "After you file the claim, you can stock up on supplies. When you return, I will go into Paradise and hire some trustworthy men as guards."

"But we have to go together," Mercy protested. "How else can we file the claim with all four names?"

"There is no time to waste. You file the claim in your name first. We can transfer shares into our names after we hire guards. Is that all right with you, Frosty?"

"Sure." He winked at Mercy. "Guess I can trust her."

"We should head on back to camp and turn in," Edward said. "The sun will be up before we know it."

"What about him?" Mercy darted a wary glance toward the skeleton.

Frosty cackled again. "What about him? He ain't going nowhere."

"Should we . . . should we . . . remove him?"

Edward rubbed the back of his neck. "We will decide what to do in the morning. He has been resting in this tunnel for many, many years. Another night will not hurt."

He was right, of course. The skeleton frightened her silly, but the thought of leaving him there bothered Mercy. "We should bury him at the mission."

"That is a good idea."

"You're not just saying that?" she queried Edward, doubting his sincerity. He had, after all, accused her of being irrational.

"No. It makes sense. He once lived there."

That settled, they made ready to leave the mine.

Edward went first. Climbing onto the rock base, he scaled the ridge with ease. Once on top, he knelt at the edge and reached down to her.

"Just a minute," Mercy called to him and paused at the opening. Moments ago, she'd been eager to leave the mine and the frightening skeleton behind. Now, she hesitated, the significance of the situation finally sinking in.

"Something wrong?" Frosty asked, concern in his raspy voice.

Mercy felt tears sting her eyes. "My father gave up his life to find this mine."

"Charles was a good man. The best friend an old coot like me could've had." Frosty put a hand on Mercy's damp cheek. "If he were alive today, he'd be mighty proud of you."

"He tried hard to do the right thing, didn't he?"

"He did indeed. Maybe he didn't always succeed, but he tried. And he loved you to pieces."

Frosty's words managed to ease a large portion of the pain squeezing Mercy's heart. Giving him a feeble smile, she ducked and went through the opening, following Edward up the ridge with considerably less agility than he'd demonstrated. By the time she reached the top, her tears had dried and she felt once more in control of her emotions.

Edward pulled her over the side and onto her feet with such little effort, she might have been a rag doll. She swayed momentarily, and he wrapped an arm around her waist to steady her.

"Let me go," she demanded when he continued to hold her longer than circumstances necessitated.

She was immediately reminded of the first time they'd met in the mine shaft—the day Samson had been brought up from the lower levels. Then, as now, her heart underwent the most peculiar palpitations. She had to remind herself that she and Edward were no longer courting, but a part of her reveled at the feel of his strong embrace and longed to stay there.

The rest of her life, perhaps?

No! She must stick to her guns at all costs. Had she not just this afternoon called off their courtship? And with good reason.

"Thank you for helping me, but as you can see, I'm fine."

"*Mon pleasure.*"

Those were the same words he'd uttered to her that day in the mine shaft. Was this a plan to remind her of their instantaneous mutual attraction? If so, it was working. Their gazes held fast, never wavering. Mercy's arms crept up his shoulders despite her best intentions to glue them to her sides. He murmured something in French and though she didn't understand him, her body responded, becoming soft and malleable.

Edward drew her closer, his head bent as if to kiss her. She absolutely, positively must tell him to stop what he was doing.

"*Chère.*"

Her lips parted with a sigh.

"Hey! Anyone there?" Frosty called from below. "I'm waiting for a little help."

Shock set in. Mercy gave a small yelp and pushed Edward away, her sanity returning. Thank goodness Frosty had interrupted them when he did. She'd almost let Edward kiss her. What a mistake that would have been. The day's events had obviously rattled her in more ways than one.

To her annoyance, Edward smiled knowingly, then knelt to give Frosty a hand up. For one brief second, she entertained the notion of planting the sole of her boot in Edward's hind end and shoving with all her might.

She resisted.

Some minutes later, the three of them reached the bottom of the foot path. The short walk to camp felt like a ten-mile hike. Every muscle in Mercy's tired body ached. Her head throbbed from when she'd hit the tunnel wall, and her bandaged hands had gone numb. The worst injury, however, had been to her heart. She didn't think it would ever heal properly.

Luiz bounded over to greet them the moment they came into view and fired question after question at them. "*Senorita* Bidwell, are you all right? What took so long? Did you find the mine?"

"Yes, Mercy found it."

The boy whooped and cheered and threw himself at Edward, who picked him up and slung him onto his back.

Mercy did her best to ignore the charming scene. All she wanted was to sleep.

When the chance finally came, she dropped off immediately, only to rouse a few hours later. Exhausted, yet fully awake, she tossed and turned on the hard ground, her mind a maelstrom of thoughts and images. Things weren't supposed to happen this way. Yesterday should have been the best day of her life, but in some ways, it was the worst.

She'd found the Silver Angel Mine. In her many dreams, no matter the version, she lived happily ever after from here on in. That didn't appear likely.

Her father was dead, possibly murdered, and she'd never see him again. She owned a share of the mine, but if what her uncle said was true, it would require every penny the silver coins brought, and then some, to fund the reopening of the mine. Leaving Paradise and traveling was out of the question until the mine started producing, possibly years from now. Unless she sold her share, which she had to admit presented a certain appeal.

And lastly, the man she thought she'd marry had betrayed

her. At least, it felt like betrayal, though her mind was developing an annoying tendency to disagree with her emotions.

Lying on her side, she folded an arm under her head and let the tears leak from her eyes. The mine suddenly meant very little to her. She'd found the monetary wealth she always longed for, but at a personal cost far greater than she'd ever imagined—a lifetime of happiness with the man she loved.

Chapter Eleven

January 7, 1915

*T*here isn't much to do around the campfire at night—
other than contemplate the stars, play a game of cards,
write in this journal, or talk. While I was in the mood
to star gaze, Frosty felt inclined to converse. Since I
could do both simultaneously, I indulged him, and it
ended up being quite an enlightening discussion.

We started out debating the usual; the potential outcome of our current search, where we'll search next,
the latest goings-on in Paradise, and politics. Just
when I thought he was nodding off, he asked me what
I would do if we ever found the mine. I admit to being
dumbstruck. Truth be told, I have never considered any
existence beyond searching for it.

Frosty took my lack of response as an invitation to
elaborate on all the marvelous ways in which he'd
spend his share of the money; everything from a new

automobile to a transatlantic sailing trip. I can't quite picture him living the high life, but I refrained from saying as much. We are all entitled to dream.

When he finished, I began to tell him I would probably sell my share and return to Boston, then bit my tongue, for that would be lying. Oh, I might visit Boston briefly in order to see Mercy, but I'd never stay.

The desert has become my home and, God willing, I'll spend the remainder of my days here, either as a wealthy mine owner or a penniless old fool, forever seeking a treasure that doesn't exist.

Charles Oliver Bidwell

"All's secure on the northern side, Mr. Cartier."

"Thank you, Pony." Edward smiled at the young miner he'd hired as one of three guards. He'd chosen wisely. Pony and the others had proven their trustworthiness on more than one occasion. Claim jumpers weren't so much a problem as curiosity seekers and thieves. All wanted a piece of the Silver Angel Mine. The one difference lay in the size of the piece they wanted.

"I came up here to tell you there's a fellow in camp asking for you. Says he's one of them reporters from *The Phoenix Chronicle*." Pony was clearly impressed.

"Is that so?" Edward glanced at camp, easily visible from the mesa, especially now that it was swarming with people. A row of tents divided the camp in half, neat as a picket fence. Smoke from three separate fires billowed upward and dissipated on the breeze. "What does he want?"

"To interview you and Miss Bidwell, or so he says. If you ask me, he won't be the last. This here mine is news."

Edward couldn't disagree. Not ten minutes after Mercy filed the claim, half of Paradise had already heard about it.

That word had reached Phoenix was no surprise. "Thank you, Pony. I will head down in a minute."

The younger man tugged on the brim of his hat, then slung his rifle hard against his shoulder. Looking imposing despite his lack of years, he said, "Be dark in a couple hours. I'll check back with you before Johnnie Johnson relieves me." Pivoting smartly on his heels, he made for the footpath leading down the ridge.

Edward watched him go, then turned his attention to the two men climbing over the ledge, one a geologist and the other an engineer.

To make entry in and out of the mine easier, Edward and Frosty had moved the rock base and replaced it with a short ladder. They'd also buried the skeleton at the mission. Luiz even fetched the old priest from *Rio Concho* so that the appropriate prayers were intoned over the grave.

Had that been only yesterday? So much had happened in the week since Mercy found the mine. Edward still had trouble believing the story about the fox, but wasn't one to question good fortune. Real or not, it had led Mercy to the greatest discovery of the decade and made them, if not rich, at least famous.

"Good afternoon." Edward greeted the approaching men. Both lugged equipment and both wore knapsacks bulging with strange looking paraphernalia.

"Hello, Mr. Cartier."

The scientists were a necessary expense and one Edward, Mercy, and Frosty had unanimously agreed on. The geologist would tell them how much ore was in the mine. The engineer would tell them how best to get it out, and how much the operation would cost.

Money had become a critical issue. As it turned out, the silver coins were worth more than Frosty's estimation. The assayer had certified their value at twenty-two hundred, forty-seven dollars. Several hundred of those dollars had already been spent and additional costs were rolling in at a rate that made Edward's head spin.

Luckily, Artemis Bidwell had come through on his promise to promote Edward, or else he wouldn't be able to send his family the money they needed. He didn't quite understand the mine superintendent's change in position. In his mind, Edward hadn't fulfilled his end of their agreement and didn't deserve the promotion. But Artemis Bidwell disagreed and insisted Edward take the job, which started on Monday. The mine's discovery had enthralled just about everyone in Paradise, including, apparently, Artemis Bidwell.

"Well, I think we're about done here, wouldn't you say?" The engineer looked at his companion, who nodded in agreement.

"We might need to come back in the morning for a bit." The geologist re-packed a piece of equipment that, to Edward's inexperienced eyes, resembled a camera. "But the field work is more or less complete."

"How soon until we have the results?"

The two men shuffled their feet. "You understand, Mr. Cartier, these things take time. There are tests to run, reports to write."

"A rough guess," Edward pressed, irked by their evasiveness.

"Two weeks. Three at the outside," the engineer finally answered with a weak smile.

"No sooner?" It seemed an unbelievably long time.

"Patience, Mr. Cartier."

Easy for him to say. He didn't have money going out faster than it was coming in. "I look forward to hearing from you."

"Count on it."

Edward escorted the scientists down the footpath. At the bottom, he spied Thomas and Guillermo coming toward them. Bidding the other men farewell, he greeted his friends, glad for an excuse to stall the reporter waiting to interview him.

"*Amigo.*" Guillermo elbowed Thomas in the ribs, a huge grin splitting his sun-darkened face. "Do you think the *señor* will speak to us now that he is a rich man?"

Thomas sniffed indignantly. "Once they get a little money in their pockets, they forget who you are. Pony almost didn't let us by."

"It is good to see you." Edward grinned broadly, clapping them on their backs. "And consider yourselves lucky. There are plenty who did not get past Pony."

"Yeah, we ran into Mort Carmichael on the road," Thomas said, looking sheepish. "He was pretty mad Pony chased him off."

"Pony is a good judge of character," Edward said, and they all three laughed.

"*Señor* Bidwell told us you were taking some time off work, but he didn't say how long."

"So we figured we'd come around and find out for ourselves," Thomas finished.

"I am glad you did, very glad." Edward hadn't realized how much he missed his job. "Can I show you around?"

Thomas's face brightened. "If that means you'll let us see the Silver Angel Mine, sure!"

They'd no sooner started up the footpath when Mercy hailed Edward. He stopped short and turned to see her beckoning him with a wave.

"Edward. Can you spare a minute?"

He hesitated, taking in the fancy-dressed man with her.

"Who's that?" Thomas drawled, his usually beady eyes wide and curious.

"I think he is a reporter from Phoenix. Pony told me he wanted to interview me."

"A reporter!"

Guillermo removed his battered hat and bowed deeply in a mock show of respect. "You are famous now, *amigo*. This man will probably take your picture and put it in the newspaper. Everyone in Arizona will know who you are."

Edward grumbled at the jest, which had a ring of unappealing truth. A pang of nostalgia hit him hard in the chest. What had happened to his life? Two months ago he'd been a simple man leading a simple existence. Then Mercy entered the picture and with her, a whole string of complications.

To say he wished for things to return to the way they were wasn't entirely accurate. In fact, it was entirely inaccurate. He was eager to start his new job. They had only until the end of the month to finish the tunnel and earn their bonus. He was committed to visiting his family for Christmas and bringing Jacqueline back with him to Paradise. And if asked to choose between finding the Silver Angel Mine or marrying Mercy, he'd have picked Mercy without a moment's indecision.

Edward regretted his inept handling of their argument. Mercy had been right. No matter how well placed his intentions were, they didn't excuse his actions. He'd tried to talk with her about it off and on over the last week, but she managed to change the subject whenever he brought it up. Now, with so much enthusiasm over the mine, it didn't appear they were ever going to get the chance to resolve their differences.

Indicating the reporter with a tilt of his head, Edward told his friends, "I had best talk with him. You go on up. The mine is probably empty, the engineer and geologist just left. I will join you as soon as I am finished."

"Take your time." Thomas nudged Guillermo and the two men all but tripped over each other in their haste to see the Silver Angel Mine. "Don't hurry on account of us."

Edward didn't. He dragged his feet every inch of the way to where Mercy and the reporter waited.

"This is Phillip Mayhan of *The Phoenix Chronicle*," Mercy introduced them as Edward drew near.

"How do you do, Mr. Cartier. It's quite an honor to finally meet you." He pumped Edward's hand. "Your partner, Miss Bidwell, has been a gracious hostess, and I appreciate her taking the time to talk with me. I'm hoping you'll grant me the same consideration."

Edward would have preferred snubbing the man, but his overt friendliness made it difficult. "Certainly. I have a few minutes."

"Thank you." Phillip Mayhan opened a notebook to a clean page and removed the pencil he'd secured between pages. Licking the lead tip, he poised it above the paper, ready to write. "What, specifically, is your relationship with Miss Bidwell? Our readers want to know."

Edward stiffened at the reporter's direct question. What business was their relationship to anyone? He risked a glance at her. A blush stained her cheeks and neck. Good. He wasn't the only one suffering.

"We are partners."

"Just partners?"

Edward directed his answer to Mercy. "For the moment." She glowered at him.

Phillip Mayhan grinned and scribbled in his notebook. "I thought maybe there was more to the story."

The rest of his questions weren't nearly so personal, focusing on their adventures—and misadventures—leading up to the mine's discovery.

"I'd like to visit the mine, if that's possible." His expression shone with hope. "And take some photographs."

Edward shrugged. "I suppose. Is that all right with you?" he asked Mercy.

"Of course."

"Then I will meet you here first thing in the morning." Edward nodded brusquely at the reporter. "If you will excuse me, I have some people waiting for me at the mine."

"I don't mean to impose, Mr. Cartier, but may I accompany you? It'll give me a chance to examine the layout and check the light before I take the photographs tomorrow."

Edward wasn't sold on the idea, but agreed after seeing Mercy's enthusiastic response. Unlike him, she apparently liked notoriety. "All right. Follow me."

"What were you thinking?" she hissed under her breath as they hiked the footpath. "That remark about being more than partners was completely out of line." She darted a quick glance over her shoulder at Phillip Mayhan. "Heaven only knows what he'll put in the newspaper article."

"It is getting dark sooner these days," Edward said, pulling the same trick on her that she'd pulled on him all week.

"Don't think you can change the subject."

He flashed her a wide smile. "I just did."

With a toss of her honey-brown hair, she cut in front of him and forged ahead. He enjoyed the view of her from that angle immensely.

At the top, she turned and indicated for Phillip Mayhan to follow her. "Right this way, and watch your step. The ladder's a bit rickety."

Mercy descended first, then the reporter. Edward held the top of the ladder to steady it for them.

"Thomas! Guillermo! You in there?" he called over the side. When his friends didn't answer, he became concerned. He hoped they didn't do something foolish, like decide to explore the series of winding tunnels stretching back into the mountain.

When Mercy and Phillip Mayhan were safely on the ledge, Edward started down. "Wait for me," he instructed, but they didn't listen, ducking under the ladder and disappearing into the mine.

Miffed, and not entirely sure why, he climbed down the old ladder, which groaned and creaked under his weight. He shouldn't be angry. Mercy had discovered the mine and was part owner of it. She had every reason to show it off.

The lack of voices bothered him. Phillip Mayhan didn't strike Edward as the type to be awed into silence. Flattening himself against the rock wall, he crouched, his boots making a scuffling sound as he scooted through the opening.

On the other side, he stood up and blinked until his eyes adjusted to the dim light. Then he stepped fully into the main tunnel.

The sight greeting him wasn't what he expected, and didn't immediately register. Mercy knelt beside Phillip Mayhan's prone body, but her gaze was fixed on Edward. Her mouth fell open as if to scream. Nothing came out.

"Mercy?"

A man emerged cautiously from the shadows.

Before Edward could move, someone grabbed him from behind and jerked him backwards, knocking him off his feet. Unprepared, he landed against his assailant. A strong arm encircled his neck and tightened with the force of a steel vice, forcing him to his knees. He fought violently, digging his fingers into the heavily muscled arm imprisoning him.

When the cold, hard barrel of a pistol was shoved into the side of his neck, he went stone still. The click of a trigger being cocked filled his ears, loud as a clap of thunder.

Good God, this can't be happening!

The individual holding him, the dependable crew member Edward had also considered a good friend, growled in a low, lethal voice. "Move one inch, and your next breath will be your last."

* * *

"Please, Lord," Mercy murmured a hoarse prayer, "don't let him shoot Edward."

Her muddled brain tried to absorb the nightmarish scene unfolding before her and make sense of it.

"What do you want, Guillermo?" Edward demanded in a strained voice, his forehead damp with sweat.

"Only what is due me, *amigo*." Guillermo's lips curled into a sneer. "The *Angel de Plata*."

"The mine?" Mercy inhaled sharply. "You want the mine?"

"No!" Edward began struggling again. He stopped abruptly and threw back his head when Guillermo drove a knee into his ribs. Pain clouded his features, then anger.

"It belongs to me," Guillermo roared, "and I will have it."

"That's preposterous." Mercy shot to her feet. "The Silver Angel belonged to no one until we found it."

"The Rodriguez family claimed it years ago and paid for it with their lives." Guillermo's features twisted into a furious mask that in no way resembled the happy-go-lucky miner they all knew. "I should have been the one to find it. And I would have, were it not for your father."

"My father!" It felt like the ground rippled beneath Mercy's feet, leaving her dizzy and shaking. "What does he have to do with any of this?" Even as she asked the question, excerpts from her father's journal flashed in her mind's eye. "You knew my father!" she accused him.

"I knew him." Guillermo spat on the ground. "I curse the day he set foot in our house."

Mercy involuntarily retreated. There was so much hatred in the man, she didn't doubt for an instant that he'd kill Edward if it suited him. She had to do something, but what? Overpowering him wasn't an option. He'd pull the trigger if she made one wrong move. Screaming was also pointless. Help would arrive too late to be of any use.

"Why?" Thomas asked, signs of confusion on his face. "What did Miss Bidwell's father ever do to you?"

She turned to stare at the other miner, having forgotten all about his presence despite his nearness. He stood quietly on the other side of Phillip Mayhan's prone body.

"You really do not know?" Guillermo appeared offended at their ignorance.

"No," Mercy answered. "Should we?"

Guillermo looked at her with the same contempt he had shown young Luiz at the company party so long ago. "I am disappointed. Your father mentions me often in his journal."

"How would you—" Mercy's hand flew to her mouth. All this time, it was him! "You stole the journal from my room."

"Stupid woman. All of you are stupid," he shouted. "Leaving bedroom windows open and warehouse doors unlocked. You made it much too easy for me."

"You vandalized the wagon, too!"

His laugh rang with condescension. He was, Mercy understood with chilling clarity, a man without remorse.

"Did you kill my father?"

Her question, phrased more like an accusation, appeared to unsettle him. He didn't immediately respond, and his hold on Edward slackened. "I did not mean to. It was an accident."

The blood drained from Mercy's head. Had Thomas not reached a hand to her, she might have crumpled to the ground beside Phillip Mayhan.

"How could you?" Her voice cracked with emotion.

Edward swore and took an awkward, backhanded swing at Guillermo, missing him entirely.

In response, Guillermo tightened his grip on Edward so hard that he choked. Then he raised slitted eyes to Mercy. She recoiled at the disturbing glint flickering in them.

"Your father was like you, stubborn and foolish. He refused

to let me join his expedition, even though I could have provided many clues to the mine's location." Guillermo kicked
Edward in the ribs before slackening his hold. His chest
heaved from exertion. "I know many stories about the mine;
some I learned while growing up, others during my travels."

His mood suddenly changed, and he scowled. "I grow
weary of all this talk." His eyes cut to a pile of equipment
near the entrance. "Thomas, bring that rope here. Tie his feet
and hands together." With one arm, he half-dragged Edward
to the tunnel wall and leaned him against it, all the while
keeping the gun leveled at his head. "And make sure it is
tight. I do not want him escaping."

Mercy could almost hear her father's voice reciting
excerpts from his journal: *He is familiar with the country-
side and local folklore . . . In exchange, he will act as guide
and share his vast knowledge of the mine . . . If ever I met a
man with a hidden agenda, it is him.*

"Who are you?" she gasped, harboring a suspicion that
seemed too impossible to take seriously.

"Guillermo Rodriguez Gomez." His grin was malevolent.
"But your father knew me as Guillermo Houseman."

"The rancher's son." It was true!

"He gave me his name, but I was *not* his son." Guillermo
puffed up with pride. "I am a Rodriguez. Bernardo
Rodriguez was my grandfather. John Houseman married my
mother when I was a boy. He was an old man and wanted a
son to take over his ranch." Guillermo made a disgusted
sound. "I refused. Ever since I can remember, my mother
told me about the Rodriguezes and their journey from
Mexico to the *Mano del Diablo* Mountains. She said it was
my duty to find the mine and restore honor and riches to our
great family."

"If you are a Rodriguez," Thomas interjected, "then Luiz

is your cousin." He stood, having finished binding Edward's hands and feet, and went to check on Phillip Mayhan, who had yet to stir.

Guillermo seethed with unsuppressed rage. "He is no cousin of mine. He is a beggar and thief who uses the Rodriguez name to impress people."

Mercy disagreed, but said nothing for fear of antagonizing Guillermo further. Thank goodness the boy wasn't with them. He'd wanted to come, but Edward insisted he remain in Paradise and start school.

"John Houseman did not understand that my duty to my real family came before the ranch—before anything! He tried to make me into someone I was not. He forbade my mother from talking to me about the Rodriguezes or the *Angel de Plata*. Then he sold all her jewelry, including the ring my grandfather gave her. I never forgave him for that."

"Did you kill him, too?" Mercy blurted.

"No!" Guillermo bore down on her, momentarily forgetting about Edward. "And I did not kill your father. We struggled over the ring, and he fell. John Houseman had no right selling it to him. It belonged to me, and I wanted it back." He glared at her. "Now it is lost forever in the mountains."

Cowering slightly, Mercy forced herself not to reach for the ring around her neck, grateful she'd taken to wearing it tucked inside her shirt. The ring could come in handy as a bargaining tool. Guillermo obviously didn't know she had it, or that her father had somehow managed to hold onto it during the fall. She would always be grateful Frosty had recovered the ring and saved it for her.

Guillermo continued, his tone intentionally cruel. "He screamed when he fell. I just stood there and watched. When that old prospector came running, I hid."

"Coward," Mercy hissed.

"It was your father's fault he fell." Guillermo viciously jabbed the air with the gun. "He should have given me the ring." All at once, he sagged, the anger leaving him as quickly as it came. "I did not mean to kill him."

"But you will kill us?" Edward said, twisting his bound hands and feet.

Guillermo wheeled on him, the gun raised. "If I have to."

"Stop," Mercy cried out, taking a frantic step forward and then halting. "What do you want?" she asked in a calmer voice.

His head jerked around. "I told you. The *Angel de Plata*." Keeping the gun trained on Edward, he reached inside his shirt and withdrew a folded paper. Smiling, he held it out to her. "Here."

"What is it?"

"A transfer. Sign it, and I will let you all go free."

She took the paper with trembling fingers, opened it, and scanned the single page. Guillermo had already filled in the necessary information. She need simply sign it and, assuming he was a man of his word, they'd walk out of there under their own power, alive and unharmed.

"Is the transfer legal?" she asked.

"It will be, when he witnesses it." Guillermo acknowledged Thomas with a jerk of his head.

"What if I refuse?" He glared at his former buddy.

"You will not refuse, *mi amigo*." Guillermo put the point of the gun directly to Edward's right temple. "Not when she begs you to sign. And she will beg you."

"You would use your friend like this?" Disgust filled Mercy.

"I have no friends." Guillermo's smile vanished. "Now sign the transfer."

"What's to stop us from turning you over to the authorities?" she challenged, then wished she'd kept her mouth shut. She'd just given him another reason to shoot them.

"You can try, but I do not think they will believe you."

"You're crazy!"

"Am I?" His voice dropped to an intimidating level. "When that reporter wakes up, you will tell him that he hit his head on the beam over there and was knocked out. While he was unconscious, you signed the mine over to me. Being the good and kind person that you are, you decided the mine should be returned to its rightful owners, the Rodriguezes. He will print the story in his newspaper and all the other newspapers in the state will do the same. You can try to have me arrested, but no one will believe you. After all, I will have the transfer, signed and witnessed. And everyone in Arizona who has read a newspaper will think you changed your mind and are trying to get the mine back."

"What makes you think I'll go along with this plan of yours?" Mercy asked, appalled that he'd even consider something so outrageous.

"Because you want your father's journal back, yes? And that is the only way you will ever see it again."

Mercy felt like she'd been slapped in the face. "Where is it?"

"Nearby."

"I want to see it first."

"No. Not until you tell the reporter the story. And you better be convincing. If he doesn't buy every word you say, I will burn the journal."

She was tempted to offer him the ring, but some instinct told her negotiating would be futile. There was nothing stopping him from killing them all and simply taking the ring.

"If you're lying about the journal," she vowed vehemently, "I'll hunt you down myself."

"Do not threaten me or you will be very sorry." Hatred emanated from his every pore. "Now sign the transfer."

Mercy glanced at Edward over the top of the paper. He'd been uncharacteristically quiet during the exchange between her and Guillermo. Was he hoping she'd sign the transfer and save them? Or was he making peace with God in preparation for his inevitable death?

From beneath lowered lashes, she tried to read his expression. He didn't appear hopeful, nor did he appear resigned. He looked . . . preoccupied.

He caught her watching him, and she swore he mouthed the words, *do not sign*.

Do not sign? What other choice did she have?

Slowly lifting his hands, Edward placed a single finger to his lips, signaling her to be silent. When he bent his wrists, the rope binding him hung loose. Either Edward managed to untie himself, or Thomas had disobeyed Guillermo's order.

Edward pointed toward his right boot. At first Mercy didn't understand, then his meaning sank in. The knife he always carried there. The knife he knew how to use with expert skill.

Cutting a quick glance at Guillermo's back, he mouthed, *do not sign* again.

He meant to take on Guillermo!

Could he?

Edward was good with his knife and had the element of surprise, as well as help from Thomas. But Guillermo had a gun and an emotional sickness that blinded him to all things save his one demented purpose.

Did she have the right to risk their lives? Then again, did she have the right to forfeit the mine when the chance existed they might defeat Guillermo?

"What is taking so long?" he growled.

She blinked and brushed at her eyes. "I'm reading. The light in here is bad."

"Hurry," he warned.

"I don't have a pen."

"I do." He dug in his pants pocket.

During the brief distraction, Edward caught her attention and smiled his encouragement. Mercy bit her lower lip, debating.

The Silver Angel Mine, the *Angel de Plata*—How many people had died for it through the centuries? Hundreds, maybe. Indians. Priests. The Rodriguezes. Countless treasure seekers.

Her own father.

If Guillermo carried out his threat, she, Edward, Thomas, and Phillip Mayhan would become the latest casualties. Was owning the mine worth the exorbitant cost? Was any treasure? Her father would say yes. But what about Edward? She didn't think he'd agree. Conventional wealth didn't appear to matter to him. He was already a rich man. He had his family, his daughter, a home, a good job, health, friends, the respect of his fellow miners. He had many of the very things she herself craved, and had finally found. They'd been right there under her nose all along. Why hadn't she realized it before?

Her list of blessings could also include marrying a wonderful man, if she let it. She'd been wrong about Edward. He wasn't like her father at all. He loved her and was willing to risk his life for her. *Her.* Not the mine. She knew that as certainly as she knew her own name.

Oliver Charles Bidwell had spent a decade in hiding after losing his wife. Mercy vowed not to follow in his footsteps. She would embrace life, even when it dealt her a hard or unfair hand. She would not allow it to come to a meaningless end in a dark, dank tunnel.

Feeling no regret whatsoever, she held out her hand to

Guillermo and took the fountain pen he'd produced. Uncapping it, she put the tip to paper and signed her name.

Guillermo lowered his gun.

All of a sudden Edward lunged to his feet. Charging like a bull seeing red, he tackled Guillermo from behind. The two men, a tangle of arms and legs, hit the ground with a bone-crunching thud.

Chapter Twelve

February 12, 1915

*M*ercy is coming to Paradise next month. Nothing I've said thus far has dissuaded her.

I want to be angry with her because she's going against my wishes, but the truth is, I'm overjoyed at the prospect of seeing her again. It has been so long since that day I left her on the steps of the boarding school. Ten years—years that have dragged on, in one respect, and flown by in another. I probably won't recognize her.

And what will she think of me?

I'm not the man she remembers. The past decade has changed me in many ways, as I'm sure it's changed her. I'm looking forward to becoming reacquainted with my daughter. Now a woman, no longer a little girl with tangled hair and scabs on her knees.

She wants adventure, or so she writes, and thinks searching for the Silver Angel Mine will satisfy this yearning. It might. It did mine. Though my motives were *entirely different from hers. While I wished to forget the past, Mercy is excitedly anticipating the future, which pleases me enormously.*

Nothing will keep me from meeting her train. I hope with all my heart she finds whatever it is she's looking for, be it the mine, or some other treasure far more valuable than silver.

Charles Oliver Bidwell

"I could have taken him."

"I don't doubt it, Edward." Mercy sighed. "That's not the point."

She'd been able to avoid his questions all evening, but he'd finally succeeded in cornering her alone. Everyone was packing up camp and loading wagons by moonlight and firelight. Guillermo had given them until morning to vacate the area before he started shooting. Mercy had no desire for another encounter with the new owner of the Silver Angel Mine.

Phillip Mayhan hadn't waited around either. The reporter had left for Phoenix as soon as he was fit to travel, eager to scoop the other newspapers with his unbelievable story of how Mercy had signed over the Silver Angel Mine to one of the last remaining members of the Rodriguez family.

"Then why did you sign the transfer?" Edward refused to be put off. He hooked her by the elbow and spun her around when she ignored him. "I thought you were pretending in order to distract Guillermo, or I never would have pulled my knife on him."

Mercy's throat went dry at the memory of their scuffle. For several long minutes, she hadn't known which to be more afraid of: Guillermo shooting Edward, or Edward stabbing Guillermo. She'd inadvertently screamed when Edward knocked the gun from Guillermo's hand and sent it sailing across the tunnel floor. It came to a rest near Thomas, who had the presence of mind to pick it up, aim it, and say, "Take it easy, boys."

"I'm sorry you were hurt." Mercy resisted reaching up and tenderly touching the angry purple bruise on Edward's jaw. "I didn't think you'd attack him as long as I signed the transfer."

"I wanted to bury my knife in his stomach." His lips barely moved as he spoke. "And would have if Thomas had not stopped us."

She didn't doubt that. He must feel so betrayed. Guillermo had fooled him—fooled everyone—completely, and that probably didn't sit well with Edward. When he gave his affection, be it to family or friends, he did so fully and without reservations. She knew, because for a short period of time, she'd been the recipient of that affection. And she'd be a liar if she said she didn't still crave it.

After their brief interlude at the rock wings last week, when she'd found the Silver Angel Mine, she was convinced he felt the same. If they were to resume their courtship, one of them would have to make the first move. Mercy didn't think she had the nerve for such a bold step. Edward had a way of leaving her emotions in pandemonium. In his close company, she tended to act more like a naive schoolgirl than the confident adult woman she considered herself to be.

"It wasn't worth the risk," she said. Heat built where his hand clamped her arm, spreading along the length of it. "No amount of money is."

His brows arched. "We can still go to the authorities if you want."

She thought of her father's journal, wrapped in a blanket and safely secured in the back of the wagon. With its return, a calming peace had settled over her. It occurred to her that having the journal back meant more to her than losing the mine. "The Silver Angel has claimed enough lives. I won't be responsible for any more."

He studied her critically. There was approval in his voice when he said, "You have changed these past months."

"Yes," she answered thoughtfully. "I suppose I have."

Mercy's heart started its typical fluttering as the atmosphere between them became charged with electricity. Then it skipped erratically when his fingers slid up her arm to close over her shoulder. In defense, she withdrew. The situation was highly inappropriate for any intimacies.

"We'd best finish packing before Guillermo comes down the ridge firing on us."

"Will you save me again, Mercy, like you did in the mine? Perhaps throw yourself in front of me when he starts shooting?"

"Don't be ridiculous," she trilled, giving herself away and letting him know how much his touch affected her. "That isn't going to happen."

His fingers caressed her shoulder. "I think I like the idea of you protecting me, instead of the other way around."

"I plan on being long gone before it comes to that."

"You two arguing or wooing?" Frosty said, chuckling as he led Samson and Buttercup from the pen to the wagon.

Mercy would have jumped a foot in the air if Edward wasn't holding her. Acutely embarrassed at being caught in what could be construed as an embrace with Edward, she tried to put a respectable distance between them. Edward would have none of it. Fortunately, the darkness partially hid them.

"We're not arguing," she answered hotly.

"Could've fooled me." Something rustled as Frosty dug around in the wagon bed. "All you two ever do is fight. That, and make cow eyes at each other." He grunted, lifting a heavy harness out and carrying it to Samson. "When you finally figure out how you really feel, be sure and let me know."

"I already know." Edward's voice was like silk. "What about you, Mercy?"

His eyes, dark and probing, were the first thing she'd noticed about him. And then, as now, she thought they could see straight through her.

He'd spared her from making the first move by doing it himself. That left it up to her to respond. How she responded would dictate what happened next and, quite possibly, the many years to come.

Her heart abruptly ceased its fluttering. She made her decision. The woman who had stepped off the train at the Paradise station would never reveal her feelings to a man. Especially not in front of other people.

But she wasn't that woman anymore. This Mercy Bidwell went after what she wanted. "I didn't save you from the clutches of death just to lose you."

"Say it," he insisted, gripping her now with both hands and lifting her onto the balls of her feet.

"I love y—"

His mouth came crashing down on hers in a searing kiss unlike any of the previous ones they'd shared. Frosty's satisfied laughter faded into the background. As did the stars, the campfires, and any other distractions.

After an endless moment, Edward broke away to plant a line of tiny kisses down the side of her neck. Between each one, he murmured, "*Je t'aime, mon chéri*," over and over.

When he drew her more fully into his arms, she didn't fight him. Standing on tiptoes, she returned his ardor measure for measure.

"Marry me," he said, his breath ragged. He threaded his fingers through her hair and held her head between his hands.

It took Mercy a few seconds to realize he wasn't speaking French. Tears filled her eyes, and she nearly burst with joy. In the span of two hours, she'd gone from being afraid for their lives to the prospect of a glorious future. How strange the fates were, and how kind. She'd been granted her dearest wish—not the Silver Angel Mine, but Edward.

"Yes! I'll marry you."

He picked her up and swung her around in a circle, then set her down and kissed her soundly once more.

"I could use a little help here," Frosty hollered. "That is, if you're through proposing."

They flashed guilty smiles at each other, then dissolved into laughter. Something moved in the distance, capturing Mercy's attention. A shaft of particularly bright moonlight arrowed down from night sky, bathing the rock wings in an unearthly glow. She'd never seen anything so beautiful, or so inspiring. No wonder the mine had been named the Silver Angel.

A small gasp escaped her. "Look."

Edward followed her gaze. "Magnificent."

"Isn't it?"

The breeze picked up, tossing her hair and cooling her heated cheeks. As before, Mercy swore she could hear her father's voice, encouraging her, guiding her.

This time, however, he was bidding her farewell.

"Goodbye," she whispered, her fingers clasping the ring around her neck. The cold metal instantly warmed in her palm.

"What did you say?" Edward asked, turning toward her.

"Nothing." She slipped her hand into his, feeling the happiest she'd ever felt since before her mother died.

"You are certain you are not sorry about losing the mine?"

"No." They began strolling back toward the wagon. "Not sorry at all."

The platform shook beneath their feet as the train came to a screeching stop in front of the Paradise station. Steam shot out from under the engine's great, black body in giant plumes, raining minuscule drops of hot moisture on anyone standing nearby.

Luiz kicked at a knot in the wooden plank with the toe of his shoe and said sulkily, "I want to go with you."

"You must stay here and attend school." Edward patted the boy's head.

In spite of the chilly December weather, Luiz was hatless. His small ears were a vivid crimson, matching his cheeks. Mercy had instructed him to put on a hat before leaving the house, but he'd resisted. She didn't think he meant to be disobedient as much as he was protesting their leaving without him. He wanted to go, and she didn't blame him. She herself could hardly wait.

The idea of traveling to another country had Mercy skipping with excitement. Their journey would take them across a large portion of the United States before crossing over into Quebec. She'd seen much of the country when she'd ridden the train from Boston to Paradise, but this trip would take a different route, with different stops. And she wouldn't be alone. Her husband of four weeks would be with her.

Mercy smiled to herself. The heady sensation of being newly married had not yet worn off. She had only to look at Edward, tall and handsome in his suit, and she fell in love all over again.

Their wedding had been well attended, both because of Uncle Artemis's position in the community and the many miners Edward worked with. Thomas had served as

Edward's best man. He would have been there today to see them off, but his recent promotion to assistant foreman required him to cover for Edward at the mine.

As Mercy had predicted, they'd received numerous gifts—enough to turn their new house into an attractive, cozy home. Edward felt they needed more room, what with Jacquelyn, Luiz, and the other children they hoped to have. And with his new job, they could afford something larger.

"I don't like school." Luiz continued to kick at the knot.

"It ain't all that bad." Frosty playfully yanked the boy's collar. He'd left his winter camp to come see the newlyweds off, saying he wouldn't miss it for the world. "Heck, I went to school for three years myself. I'll help you with your homework if you want."

That would be something to see, thought Mercy, covering her giggle with a cough. Edward appeared to be having similar trouble containing his amusement.

Lowering himself to Luiz's level, he took the boy by the arms. "I know this is hard for you, son. You have never gone to school. But you must learn to read and write. How else can you become a foreman like me?"

"I will miss you," Luiz cried and threw his arms around Edward. "Six weeks is a long time."

"We will miss you, too." He stroked the boy's back. "The Ketchems are nice people. They will take good care of you."

Sara Jane's parents had generously offered to house Luiz. Mercy had always liked the elder Ketchems, but since Edward didn't get along with Mort Carmichael, their brand new son-in-law, the offer had come as a surprise. Aunt Connie had explained that Mrs. Ketchem felt despondent over her only daughter moving out of the house. And since Luiz and their youngest son had become friends at school, the arrangement made sense.

Mercy and Edward agreed, especially when Aunt Connie promised to keep tabs on Luiz as well.

"Will you write?" he murmured into the front of Edward's wool jacket.

"Of course."

"And telephone when you arrive," Aunt Connie said, her eyes misty as she hugged Mercy. "I swear I won't have a decent night's sleep until I'm certain you've arrived safely."

"She isn't joking," Uncle Artemis grumbled. "For both our sakes, please telephone. I can only tolerate her pacing the halls for so long."

"Do you have everything?"

"For the hundredth time, yes." Mercy laughed and separated herself from her aunt, feeling an emotional tug.

She and Edward had spent the last week packing, closing the house, and getting things in order before their departure. Tucked inside a concealed pocket in the lining of his coat, Edward carried a substantial bank note. Between the bonus he'd earned for completing the tunnel and what remained of the silver coins they'd found, there was more than enough money to pay for their passages. The remainder would go to the Cartiers to see them through the winter.

Only last week, Edward's brother, Rene, had written to report good news. Their sister, Emmeline, had married Anne-Marie's twin brother, Aubert. He'd moved in with the Cartiers and had taken over the farm. Jean was staying in school, much to Rene's relief. Their father still suffered from rheumatism, but otherwise, the family was doing well.

Edward had expressed pleasure at his sister's union. He spoke highly of Aubert, who, by his account, was good natured and hard working. The marriage also reunited the two large families, neighbors and friends for many, many years.

The train whistle blew, and the conductor walking the platform hollered, "All aboard! Train departs in fifteen minutes!"

"We'd best hurry," Mercy said, giving Frosty a quick peck on his whiskered cheek. "Take care of Samson for me."

Under Frosty's care, the mule had thrived. He no longer limped. His former dull coat gleamed in the morning sun. And though blind, he got around nearly as well as a sighted animal.

"Give him plenty of apples," she added.

"I will, I will." Frosty pinched her chin between his thumb and forefinger, his rheumy eyes unusually bright. "You'd best skedaddle before you miss your train."

Mercy walked into her uncle's outstretched arms.

He nearly crushed her with the force of his hug. "I love you, sweetpea," he said in her ear. "Hurry home."

"I love you, too, Uncle. Thank you for everything." It hurt to swallow with such a painful lump in the back of her throat.

He set her back from him and in a scratchy voice said, "Before you leave, I have something for you and Edward. Sort of a bon voyage present."

"Uncle, you've done so much."

"Well, I'm simply the messenger. Edward, come and take a look."

Uncle Artemis extracted an envelope from his coat pocket. "This arrived yesterday. I hope you don't mind that I opened it."

"What is it?" Mercy asked, taking the envelope.

"A report from those scientists you hired."

"But we cancelled our contract with them." Edward peered over Mercy's shoulder as she removed a sheet of paper.

"Yes. But when I wrote them about Guillermo and the unscrupulous way he came to own the Silver Angel Mine, they decided to finish the report and send it to you." He tapped the paper. "I think you'll see why."